ALSO BY CHARLES D. HAYES

FICTION

A Mile North of Good and Evil

The Call of Mortality

Portals in a Northern Sky

Pansy: Bovine Genius in Wild Alaska

Stalking Cindy

Moose Hunter Homicide

NONFICTION

September University:
Summoning Passion for an Unfinished Life

Existential Aspirations:
Reflections of a Self-Taught Philosopher

In Defense of Liberal Ideas

The Rapture of Maturity:
A Legacy of Lifelong Learning

Training Yourself:
The 21st Century Credential

Beyond the American Dream:
Lifelong Learning and the Search for
Meaning in a Postmodern World

Proving You're Qualified: Strategies for
Competent People without College Degrees

Self-University: The Price of Tuition Is the
Desire to Learn. Your Degree Is a Better Life

BENZEERILLA

BY CHARLES D. HAYES

AUTODIDACTIC PRESS

Autodidactic Press
575 S. Begich Drive, Wasilla, AK 99654
www.autodidactic.com
info@autodidactic.com
autpress@alaska.net
autpress@outlook.com
autpress@gci.net

ISBN 978-0-9885795-7-6
Printed in USA

First Edition

Book design: BookWiseDesign.com
Source cover image: Rast / 123RF Stock Photo

Publisher's Cataloging-in-Publication
(Provided by Quality Books, Inc.)

Hayes, Charles D. (Charles Douglas)
  Benzeerilla / Charles D. Hayes.
  pages cm
  LCCN 2017906633
  978-0-9885795-7-6 (paperback)
  978-0-9885795-9-0 (ebook)

  1. Transgenic animals--Fiction. 2. Apocalyptic
fiction. 3. Science fiction. I. Title.

PS3608.A92B46 2017   813'.6
                  QBI17-777

From the beginning of our time on earth, man has been haunted by spine-chilling possibilities in the dark, deep corridors of his imagination. Fictional monsters such as Minotaur, Wendigo, Medusa, and Frankenstein remain larger than life in our literature. Yet real advancements in science promise to surpass our fiction and breach the moral boundaries that have guided us up to the present day.

Now comes Benzeerilla.

The Revelation

Standing erect at 8'6", the enormous figure bent forward at the waist to clear the elevator door. Everyone who looked at the spectacle gasped, froze in place, and searched the dark corridors of their minds for something sturdy to hold on to, something stable, something believable. Had they been asked, most everyone close enough to observe the scene would have agreed that the news bulletins had been right: This was a horrific blasphemy against all human rationale of science and morality.

Three security officers stepped out ahead of what appeared to be a platoon of peace officers to clear the way, big men who looked like children fleeing to keep from being stepped on by a giant. A janitor hurrying to exit the room tripped when an officer stepped on his foot, causing him to fall and spill a bucket of mop water. The colossal figure reached down and put the man on his feet as effortlessly as picking up a used paper cup that had missed the wastebasket. Once the janitor was on his feet, a hand the size of a baseball glove seized the security officer's shoulder and a voice so deep and jarring it could echo said, "You should apologize."

In the room, twelve United States senators and twenty-four congressmen were seated at conference tables. Vice President Abrams sat by himself behind a small counter normally used as a bar for serving drinks. Behind him sat a dozen members of the press. Miniscule ripples of astonishment swept through the room like a handful of gravel thrown into a pond, shocked utterances in staccato whispers—Jesus! Oh, my God! No!—followed by muffled shrieks. Then hushed silence. No one moved, no one spoke. But after a few minutes, people began to squirm and pick at their clothing, look at their hands, or search other faces for reactions, wanting relief, something to explain the unexplainable.

The guest took a seat facing the group and scanned the room. His eyes focused on a woman with auburn hair sitting by herself near a wall. Smiling at him, hers was a friendly face in a room of hostile cynics. The specially built oversized chair was so large it looked as if it belonged in an art exhibit. Abrams nodded to Senator Maynard Jackson, the committee chairman, who looked away to avoid eye contact with the visitor.

Glancing down, Jackson noticed his wrists pressing hard into the table. The fingers gripping his gavel were ghost white, drained of blood. Never in his life had he been at such a loss for words. Words were his life, but he simply didn't know what to say. For the first time ever, he dreaded hearing his own voice, knowing that the tremor of fear he felt would reveal itself when he spoke. Nothing but nothing in his stellar rise in politics had prepared him for this. He was trying to recall the first time he had heard the expression, "What would Benzeerilla say?"

Millions of dollars in Interface media had been spent posing that simple question without further explanation. What, indeed, could be worth such an expenditure? What could this creature possibly say that would justify a congressional hearing? But seeing this was clearly Benzeerilla, he felt confident the mystery would soon be solved. In any event, he wanted this spectacle to be over.

The Soothsayer

AUGUST 2043
PALMER, ALASKA

S eth Shepard opened his brown eye, then the blue one, and thought, "Receive." Flashing on the ceiling panel was a message: *S.S.—Biggest news of the century. We will be back on top soon with a story too incredible to be believed. A moral sacrilege. The public will be outraged beyond any issue in our lifetime. More later. A flood of encrypted briefs will be coming your way. Hopefully, we won't have to be in hiding much longer, but for security, you may not receive my messages in the order sent. Just as I have been saying, it's connected to WWBS. Stay safe. JD.*

Justin Davis was Seth's longtime assistant, whose work was often superior to his own. But for his looks, he would have been the media star. Justin, or JD for short, was only a year older than Seth, but he looked much older and readily admitted that his media presence made Interface radio his best option. Too nice to be called ugly, he was often described simply as odd-looking. JD's limited range of serious facial expressions seemed to convey the sentiment that worry should always be the order of the day. But if

JD said something was big, it surely was, because he was not one to exaggerate. It was more like him to understate the case. For a time, Justin had an avatar news service that looked promising at first but never captured enough audience to take off. His latest venture, TELLJD, had become the go-to place for whistle-blowers to tell all.

In the early 2030s, Seth had been riding high as a media celebrity—a freelance news producer and occasional guest news anchor with major networks, some with as many as 46 million regular viewers globally. Seth had often captured three times the audience of rival networks, while his Interface social media presence frequently led in clips going viral.

Interface biographical information said Seth had made his bones in the late 2020s and terrible '30s with his flamboyant and outrageous on-air presentations. A typical example was his employment economics newscast in January of 2031, when he jumped up from his anchor desk and shouted, "Didn't see them coming, did you? Don't know what I'm talking about, do you?" Then he walked in a tight circle with his head down, hand under his chin, as if deep in thought. Straightening suddenly, he looked directly into the camera. "Given up, have you? It's the algorithms folks, the goddamned algorithms that most of you didn't see coming. If your job could be reasoned into a progression of logic of any kind, then a bloody app or a machine can do it. It's a no-brainer, right? Thousands of truck and taxi drivers replaced by apps. Need a doctor, a lawyer, or short-order cook? How about a doctor? Then get an app with a diagnosis capability unsurpassed in accuracy."

Of course, this was all an act. It was no mystery to the public that an app economy was killing jobs. Everybody knew it and had known it for years, but Seth's way of summarizing it for effect hit a viable nerve. The public ate it up.

From time to time, he called up telecasts of the period when he had been riding high and watched them in silence with a forlorn look on his telegenic face that no one else could see. Seth's handsome appearance was mesmerizing to some. Upon first seeing him, it could take a while to realize that his eyes were different colors, and after noticing this, it was hard for many people to stop staring. His appearance had been the bane of his existence during his school years, his good looks not yet apparent and his peculiar eyes making him the go-to kid to beat up. He was bullied until his senior year in high school, but after his skinny frame turned muscular, the transformation was like the ugly duckling becoming a swan. From then on, being the focus of media attention felt almost like revenge for his years of being tormented and taunted as "Seth-clops."

When Seth was in grade school, his house was only a block and a half from an animal shelter, and he started to work there as a volunteer after school. After a year, he was paid to clean cages and care for abandoned pets, a job he did in a way that seemed to compensate for the bullying he endured. He became so fond of animals that he felt a special kinship for simple creatures. The attachment made him overtly conscious of the well-being of all forms of life.

Moments of reflection about the past allowed Seth to forget that he was the target of assassination, that he was considered a blasphemer, and that a sect in the ungovernable territory that used to be Syria had put a hefty price on his head, literally on his head. That's what they wanted—his severed head for Interface display, to show the world what happens when you disrespect the leader of Sephtis in front of a global audience. Taking refuge in a remote sustainable shelter unit was the best way he could hide in plain sight.

Seth's personal protection service (Interface Security Services ISS) assured him it was staying current with the software to keep him safe. In the mid-2030s, software security companies began offering personal protection services after miniature drones became commonplace tools for killing people. Assassination drones, ADs, or killer drones, KDs, were the size of insects and could be laced with poison. Such homicides were so common, they weren't always considered primetime news. Many were connected to criminal activity, especially in the synthetic drug trade. The powerful psychotropic drugs now in wide use were not physically addictive in the traditional sense, but their potency was such that simply wanting them was enough to drive an insatiable demand. Nothing else available had as strong an effect on one's psyche.

The last two times Seth had left his shelter, the highly sensitive intercept units on his baseball cap had activated to ready status, but this didn't necessarily mean he was being watched. He would report and discuss the activation alert with his security representative. It was too risky not to. He had learned from experience that you do not assume your protectors are as concerned about your safety as you are.

Just now, he received a signal and accepted it, another paid, thirty-second commercial that would credit his account. These interruptions were more like public service announcements than advertising, although you did get a slight monetary compensation for watching them. They were the talk of Interface social media because this series made no sense and there were so many of them. A pure white screen with blood red lettering in all caps asked the same simple question: WHAT WOULD BENZEERILLA SAY?

Knowing JD, and having heard him speculate about the meaning of these messages, Seth was confident that's what

WWBS stood for. Intriguing. But what was even more interesting was what JD must be thinking to imagine the two of them free to be back on top, out in the open, without fear of assassination. Always feeling stalked by shadows, they had wondered if that would ever be possible again in their lifetime. How does one get a bounty lifted from one's head?

Six months ago, Seth had broken his engagement with his girlfriend of more than five years. He still hurt from the agony of the whole thing, but he was glad she wasn't involved in his current situation or adding further complications. Looking out only for himself was much easier. He thought it somewhere between amusing and existentially sad that the companion he missed most was his dog Rex, a Rottweiler who had died while he was away overseas. It seemed too soon to get another dog, so he just watched videos of Rex now and then and wondered how many people in the world were as lonely for company as he was.

The Prodigy

Benjamin Brand was no ordinary person. Born in 1986, he knew from early childhood that he would be famous someday, or maybe the correct term would be *infamous*. Either way, it was bound to happen, but there were serious bumps along the way. Benjamin's IQ was off the charts, so much so that, when he was very young, he was asked numerous times to retake IQ tests because his manner didn't support the results in the eyes of his teachers. Only those who knew him well could see through his false persona, trying to pass himself off as someone far below average. Below average he was not.

Benjamin did so poorly in school that for a time he was thought to be mentally impaired. Indeed, he was, in a sense, just not in the way his detractors thought. Ben was only himself when he was alone and in deep concentration about something, anything of interest that represented a challenge. He had no tolerance, whatsoever, for what he deemed to be trivial pursuits. If one word could best describe Ben Brand it would be *serious*. His seriousness bordered on obsession.

Lucky by birth, Ben had little appreciation for his good fortune. His father was a semiconductor mogul, and his mother came from a family of old money in banking. Ben's life was uneventful through his teen years, though not traditional. After several attempts, he stopped attending school, and his parents sought private tutoring instead. They went through five tutors until they found someone who could relate to their son and be a person that Ben admired and respected.

And so, it happened that David Cruz, a child prodigy himself, guided Benjamin from one subject to another and watched his student take each one beyond his own grasp of understanding. As David explained to the parents, Benjamin Brand was one of a kind. "There are no others in the world, at least none that I know of, who are as gifted as your son."

"But how do we channel his interests into something worthwhile?" they asked.

"That's a question I can't answer yet. Only time will tell," he said.

Time did tell, but the outcome remained a mystery for many years. On the day in 2007 when Benjamin turned twenty-one, his parents were killed in an airplane crash on their way home to celebrate his birthday. Shortly after that, the Brand estate was sold. Later, the only news of Benjamin was that he had moved to South America, David Cruz had gone with him, and Benjamin had hired three newly minted PhD students from MIT to work on a project that remained a secret. Rumor had it that Brand had become interested in DNA and genetics, but that was all anyone who would talk was willing to say. Brand's work, though, would keep rumor mills running full-time on Interface social media, and the Brand organization wasn't shy about starting rumors.

2043

Introduction to <u>TELLJD Interface</u>, the place to tell all. This is my take on where we are today and where we have been. Justin Davis. Last updated January 2043.

In 2043, the world is a very different place than the one predicted at the turn of the century. It's almost as if the 21st century is following the same pattern of the 20th. In 1929, the stock market crashed. In 2029, the market was shut down when an enormous solar flare knocked out 25 percent of the satellites circling the globe and fried so many electrical transformers that much of the world remained dark for months. The financial crisis that ensued was eclipsed only by medical emergencies, followed by looting and crime sprees. Citizens in large numbers took to the streets to protest the government's inability to cope with the cascade of emergencies and the need for distributing food and medicine.

Thereafter, liberal politicians campaigned loudly about the importance of effective government, insisting that nothing more and nothing less would be acceptable. Conspiracy theorists declared the event was evidence of the "Fourth Turning," an academic prophecy offered by two sociologists near the beginning of the century.

The crisis in banking caused by the disruption of digital communication, and the accompanying loss of data, prompted the United States president and leaders of all the developed nations in the world to put a moratorium on foreclosures. At the same time, steps were initiated to restore the electronic transfer of data and capital.

For nearly six months, battery-powered short-wave radio was the only means of communication in many rural areas. Having no electricity for weeks and months on end was far more disabling than most people would have imagined beforehand. The experience would render millions to be as cautious as the generation who had lived through the Great Depression a century earlier. Frugality was suddenly avant-garde. The lesson of going for a long period without things that people truly needed would ultimately be regarded as a brain-changer.

For a time, in some areas of the country, people wandered the streets in numbers too large to be dissuaded by the National Guard. But, after a few weeks, the Guard began parceling out substantial food rations. Slowly order was restored, though not soon enough to prevent great damage to retail infrastructure. Eight months after the first massive solar eruption, electricity was available in parts of the country for a couple of hours in the evening, at least long enough to receive some daily news reports. So many medical emergencies had occurred during the blackouts that they were no longer featured in newscasts because of the anxiety they caused. Thousands of lives were lost all over the world, so many that media refrained from using actual numbers because such reminders were deemed unproductive.

Over months that quickly turned into years, solar power improved dramatically, but there was still a shortage of every kind of battery in existence. Sewer systems backed up, water-conditioning plants failed, and hospitals operating on generators routinely ran out of fuel as no provisions had been made for long-term fuel storage or replenishment. Keeping grocery stores restocked to a pre-solar storm status proved difficult because of people's tendency to horde and because so many farming operations that had relied on GPS technology were shut down.

Not until January 2032, did the retail food sector seem to recover, but by that time, shortages of some meat and vegetable products were accepted as normal. That level of normal became possible only because 27 percent of the population now self-identified as vegetarian. Their reason for doing so was partly connected to the dark secret no one liked to talk about: the fact that only a few weeks after the solar storm, people in some parts of the world began eating pets. Any dogs, cats, livestock, or poultry left alone and unattended began to disappear. When electricity and electronic data were restored, animal-friendly organizations orchestrated a dramatic Interface campaign promoting the need for vegetarianism.

Water, already a scarce commodity in municipal reservoirs, was undrinkable in much of the United States. Even today in 2043, drinking water in most stores still costs as much as commercial beverages, and in some cases more. Compounding the difficulty of maintaining an adequate food supply has been the fact that many of the ancient aquifers are no longer able to supply water for crops. The U.S. Congress is engaged in a vitriolic battle over permitting for a water pipeline from the Great Lakes, through Las Vegas, all the way to the croplands of California. With sea levels rapidly rising, some politicians are trying to make the case that desalinization can help alleviate the situation, but most scientists scoff at the idea that enough seawater can be used to have any effect on widespread water shortages. Nevertheless, states with plenty of water, like Alaska, are gaining in population, but depleted aquifers in the country's breadbasket are causing food shortages from Iowa to California.

Elsewhere in the world, a civil war is raging in parts of China. Poor people roam the streets, armed with whatever weapons they can find to fight against inequity. Thousands of people have died, many of whom had once been affluent, causing alarm to spread everywhere in the world where great disparities of wealth exist. The war in China is simply referred to today as a war of the poor versus the rich.

The Middle East is still suffering the rise of a terrorist organization known as Sephtis, as well as fallout from two dirty bomb explosions that contained radioactive material, one in Israel, the other in Egypt. Both countries accused the other of the aggression, and both are in shambles economically. Although the damage was minimal by nuclear weapon standards, the size of the area considered uninhabitable is large enough to wreak great psychological damage. The casualties numbered only in the hundreds, but media depictions have hyped the incidents to such a degree that the dispute over the source of the bombings continues to threaten more violence.

Following the catastrophe spit forth by the sun in 2029, now often referred to as the *Prometheus event*, several developed nations all over the world experienced some form of cyber-attack on their Interface system, many from yet undetermined sources. Fortunately, most of the damage involved only temporary disruptions in electricity and the theft of cyber-currency. The worldwide scramble to insulate technology against attacks by terrorists and solar storms is still behind but is improving. Even so, lingering anxiety over impending cyber-attacks makes hoarding difficult to stop.

The biggest surprise of all about technological development is that, instead of slowing down innovation, the solar catastrophe has spurred it on. It's as if the frustration of pent-up demand by people accustomed to having myriad choices inspired more creativity, which resulted in a frenzy of new high-tech startups. People want solutions to problems of every kind, and the scramble to find them has been unprecedented.

Ironically, the most positive achievement toward lowering projections for the earth's population to more manageable numbers has been the growing popularity of virtual sex. Body suits wired for stimulation can now synchronize with software to enable one's wildest fantasies to seem more real than real. Thus, in time, the single biggest demographic comprised those unwilling to marry.

As electronic media gradually came back online, their major concerns focused on meeting basic human needs. People needed reassurance from government sources that all steps necessary to harden the electrical grid were being taken, and this continues today. Prior to the 2029 solar flare, the shrill concern of environmentalists about the rise of global warming and species extinction dominated Interface social media. But by 2033, the subject was largely forgotten because monitoring the sun had become the hottest political issue. Scientists warn us repeatedly now that the sun is merely doing what stars of its type do. The only thing we might view as abnormal is having such a long period of low solar activity for a star like the sun.

Based on actual casualties, conventional wisdom says that the electronic meltdown of 2029 was worse than the stock market crash in 1929 by several orders of magnitude. Extended unemployment benefits were in place with a promise to keep them until the economy improved substantially. By 2034, unemployment in the U.S. was still 18 percent and threatening to climb higher. Then, in 2035, legislation for a guaranteed income was enacted in America and included a Manhattan-like project to build sustainable shelters with the largest budget in the history of construction for infrastructure. The shelter units rely on pseudo-fusion reactors to protect them from solar storms.

The enactment of a guaranteed income for every American citizen in 2035 saw a tectonic shift in the role of government as it issued two kinds of electronic currency: one for needs and one for wants, with the latter being proportionally smaller. The needs currency buys food and clothing and comes with time limits. It will expire if not used, but some of the expired funds can then be used over the long term to increase one's income for wants. Wants currency is based on a tax levied against the productivity made possible by digital automation and stock market trading.

The Department of Health and Human Services has been dramatically reduced in size and reorganized into an agency primarily devoted to providing information to anyone who needs it to thrive. Online counseling is available for family problems of any kind, day and night. Ongoing forums offer discussions and guidance related to every conceivable social dilemma.

In 2032, the Department of Education was also reduced in size, while its purpose and the very reasons for its existence were changed beyond recognition. Early childhood education now includes brain-scan technology to see what parts of a child's brain are not being fully developed. Strategies for remedy follow, with all coursework requiring mastery before moving on. Likewise, adults can take tests and get coursework tailored to their individual needs.

All over the world, colleges and universities now offer online services to help anyone, anywhere, learn anything at their own pace, 24/7, 365 days a year. Degree certification has given way to performance testing and proof of actual competence. In any field, demonstrated skill takes precedence over graded tests and time served in class. At first, there were multiple lawsuits over the legitimacy of judging competence, but slowly and steadily the practice has been gaining praise and public confidence. It is now assumed that intensive lifelong learning is necessary to stay current and stay competent, regardless of one's occupation. In addition, everyone is assigned a lifelong Edbot, an Interface assistant based on algorithms that are tweaked constantly to make sure that one's areas of interest are being served and that one's educational horizons are broadened and enhanced to generate enthusiasm and creativity.

Ebots are always online, searching through trillions of data bits for anything and everything one might need to function at work or leisure, even how one might counter a friend's argument about political matters. Colleges and universities worldwide are now funded by governments and by productivity taxes on business. A virtual university can be experienced by anyone with the simple admission to a booth, a communication device, or a virtual headset. In most cases, the effect of Ebots on competency in occupations is rendering incompetence obsolete. The availability of near flawless expertise by a tireless algorithmic assistant means that mistakes and poor service depend more on attitude than lack of knowledge. Many people are engaged in occupations that they couldn't have qualified for a century before. It's just assumed now that, no matter what one's job consists of, it will be conducted via professional standards with up-to-the-minute expertise.

An artificial intelligence agency involving a network of supercomputers has taken over Interface maintenance, performing trillions of calculations and code changes in a process of perpetual updating and upgrading. The system is so sophisticated that human intervention is minor and inadequate to provide what is needed to fix computer glitches at any given time. It's as if only the system knows itself well enough to make an instant diagnosis and formulate a response and remedy. The Interface is affectionately referred by many as the Singularity, and yet, even more people use the term *singularity* in a contemptuous manner to disparage the idea of a paradigm shift so overwhelming as to mark a departure from everything before it.

From a perspective that might have occurred a half-century before, it seems that America has achieved a kind of utopia in which most social problems have been solved. The reality of social angst and contempt, however, still smolders between factions and social groups. The traditional gap between liberals and conservatives is as wide as it has ever been, and most people simply accept that there will always be people who are incapable of any worldview but a narrow one. The new American president promises that she will restore moral virtue, traditional values, and moral priorities. We shall see.

Stay informed with me, Justin Davis, at <u>TELLJD</u>, *the place to tell all.*

An Invitation

While JD's public presentations didn't work out, his Interface site for whistle-blowers, TELLJD, was a smashing success. So many messages came in from anonymous sources that it was difficult and time-consuming to separate the legitimate material from the nutcases. JD's intelligent personal assistant was an Edbot he'd named Clyde. Although Clyde was very good at sorting text, when the subject matter was whistle-blowing, the information was often so out of the ordinary that Clyde was sometimes flummoxed.

For months, someone had posted hints about a blasphemous DNA experiment underway in South America. JD dismissed these at first, but whoever was sending the messages didn't sound like a kook. Finally, he responded and soon received a plea to come to South America for a meeting that would blow the lid off one of the dastardliest deeds of science in the history of humanity. It was these outrageous claims that gave him pause—like when salesmen promise something they can't deliver and you become justifiably suspicious. Still, for every outrageous statement that came in, declarations would follow that sounded rational and even understated.

JD was tempted. If the right conditions presented themselves, he just might go. The most he could lose would be the cost of airfare. Besides, it might be a wise move to get out of the country and as far away from Seth as possible for a time.

Shadows

Seth Shepard was living in a sustainable shelter unit, better known as a "slum slot." Miles of such shelters could now be found in most major cities and in many rural communities. Sustainable shelters were titanium-reinforced rooms in the shape of shipping containers, usually measuring about 12' x 16' and strung together in rows like meandering freight trains in hill country, the twists, turns, and curves going on for miles. In the late 2030s, the shelters were society's remedy for poverty. All a person had to do to be eligible for shelter accommodations was to sign an affidavit swearing you were unavailable for traditional employment and, if you were in business, that your interests were suspended or turned over to others until further notice.

In exchange for eight to sixteen hours of community service per week or a nominal fee, one could live in a shelter rent-free. Food delivered at no cost came prepared according to medical diagnostics sent from your unit's sensors. The sensors monitored vital signs, from pulse and temperature to heart rate and vitamin and nutrition needs, 24/7. The units were powered by small quasi-fusion reactors capable of powering as many units as could be constructed, and they were hardened and self-contained for protection against electromagnetic pulse (EMP) blasts or solar storms.

The shelters were generally considered the most cost-effective way to deal with poverty and chronic unemployment. Observers were surprised to see how many people opted out of the work-force when the shelter program began. Equally surprising was how many people wanted back in, once they had been idle for a few months. Still, the shelter program was so successful that wages in the private-sector workforce were rising slowly but steadily, as more and more businesses had to compete to keep employees.

On each wall of the shelters were Interface panels for communication. If one had an X27 Interface coil-cortex implant, now considered a routine procedure, a thought command alone could produce incoming messages or initiate Interface searches from anywhere in cyberspace. Since everyone had a private sensory code, an unlimited number of people could make use of a single screen, each receiving a different signal, each seeing what others could not see unless invited. Upon signing in with facial recognition and hand-print authentication, a keyboard would appear and function as if it were one's own personal computer.

Seth hadn't been out of his shelter in a week, and he was tired of running on his treadmill for exercise. In was early morning, an hour before daybreak, so he thought this would be a good time to go for a real run. With his protective cap secure on his head, he opened the hatch, clicked it shut with a thought, and began to jog at a steady pace. The air was cool and invigorating. His shelter unit in Palmer stood about 300 yards from the Matanuska River, and the bicycle path he ran on was hidden deep in a forest of birch, aspen, and cottonwood. Every now and then, a clearing would reveal mountaintops dusted with freshly fallen snow, signaling the winter to come.

After jogging a hundred yards with no warnings, he wasn't sure if he should be relieved or worried. Attack strategists were notorious for coming up with something completely different, and if you had reason for concern, some amount of paranoia was required. Seth's was off the charts. How could it be otherwise with a million-dollar reward out for his death and an extra million for his head?

Using his implant, Seth summoned Amy, his name for his personal Edbot. One of Amy's duties was to stay abreast of security, which included criminal activity concerning targeted assassinations. When Amy had no local activity to report, he started to feel good.

Then, just when he'd decided there was nothing to worry about, a sensor on his cap began to buzz. He stopped in a clearing and slowly took a 360-degree scan of the area. The sun was beginning to break light in the east. Amy sent an alert, followed by his security sensors. He could see nothing threatening, but then, not seeing what could kill you meant nothing. Most targets of the underground murder industry never saw who or what took them out. The buzzing became a low humming sound, steady, to indicate a state of alert appropriate to an unidentified threat.

Seth began to jog again, but slower this time, and he kept turning all the way around as he ran, scanning the horizon in all directions. Suddenly he thought he heard something, then a movement to his left. There was no time to do anything but stare at the horizon. A sentry unit from his cap detached, hovered for several seconds and then slammed into a KD only three feet from his face. He stood still, looking at the spot on the ground where the spent metal remnants of one of his many defense projectiles lay, his would-be assassin's miniature killer drone still smoldering and hot to the touch. His relief at being outside vanished.

Carefully he picked up the metal bits with a pair of tweezers, put them in a plastic pouch, and ran back to his unit.

Inside, he sat for a time, his mind blank, just feeling grateful to be alive. He should have been more careful. He should have guessed they would be lying in wait for him after this much time. If mercenaries were near enough for a drone attack, they must be close by. The thought made him shudder. He could imagine nothing more frightening than decapitation.

They were always trying to come up with a new strategy, but this was just a straightforward attack. Something completely different could likely be expected soon. Seth kept wondering how he could have been so foolish not to know how easy it would be to find him. JD's friends at the CIA had helped him enter the shelter under an assumed name, but then, he still used Amy and his real medical files to keep his health in check, so maybe that was how. Twice before when he had been out of the unit, his protection service had been set at the ready. At the time, he thought it must be super-sensitive, but that was clearly not the case. He had been located. What now? It had been a while since he'd heard from JD. He would have Amy check all the surveillance cameras in the area and see if any movements might offer clues about his attackers.

Looking at a wall, he thought, "Read mail," with his implant. Amy presented a short video, and suddenly he felt nauseous. A horrific homicidal scene appeared, typical of a true-crime magazine from a century ago. There was no doubt about what he was seeing. He took a deep breath and stared at the screen.

After nearly a minute, he realized he was looking at the mangled body of his associate. Justin Davis had been butchered— no, disassembled was more like it. There was so much blood, it was not possible to tell how or by what means JD had been killed, only that it was savage and brutal. In what must have been a long ordeal, Justin's head had been severed from his body. It had been placed in front of the neck where it should be, except the head was upright in a position that showed it was not connected to the body. This surely was sent by the killers to warn Seth that they knew his location. JD had been forced to tell them, but who could blame him after what they must have put him through?

Seth sat quietly for a long time, then looked up and thought, "Messages." A moment later, a short piece arrived from JD, which he apparently had sent just before he was captured: *WWBS. I know what it means and a whole lot more. A big volley of encryption coming your way. See you soon, JD.*

The Vision

The idea began as a germ but soon became an overwhelming preoccupation. Whether it happened by chance or was pure fate, one day, while searching the Interface for scientific breakthroughs, the young Benjamin Brand discovered a write-up about the Russian scientist Ilya Ivanovich Ivanov and his lifelong obsession to mate humans with apes. What an idea—the possibilities were mind-numbing. Imagine a thinking creature with many times the strength of a human. For two consecutive weeks, Brand barely slept.

Ivanov had graduated from Kharkiv University in 1896, becoming a well-respected professor of veterinary medicine a few years later. He achieved notoriety in the field of animal husbandry by perfecting ingenious methods of artificial insemination, especially with horses. In time, his ideas about cross-breeding hybridization led him to believe that he could create a hybrid creature, a magnificent warrior impervious to pain, who could thrive on anything edible. He would help Russia create an invincible army of soldiers who could run roughshod over any foe.

Ivanov's ill-fated experiments soon tarnished his reputation as a scientist. Rumors about his disappointing results began to be regarded as a ghoulish sideshow, and he wound up in exile. Some records of his research efforts still existed, however, and these were purchased by a benefactor in South America, who insisted on receiving the original documents with verification that any remaining copies had been destroyed.

In modern times, there was talk of cloning experiments in countries where laws did not prohibit activity that most people would think of as morally blasphemous. In San Diego, a prehistoric mammoth clone had been born to an elephant, but it died soon after birth. In several locations around the world, according to hearsay, one could pay large sums to order a child à la carte, through gene manipulation for specific traits, but so far, there had been no proof of success.

In 2013, a team of American biologists did what was thought to have been impossible when they engineered an expansion of the genetic code in DNA from an alphabet of four letters to six. Speculation in scientific circles suggested that Benjamin Brand's laboratory had increased the DNA code further and perhaps even doubled it, but again there was no proof, just a lot of chatter. If it were true, it would be one of the most significant discoveries in the history of science.

Pilar

She was the youngest of three brothers and four sisters in her family. Her father often teased her small stature, saying the family had run out of Guaraco by the time they got to her. In a nutshell, Pilar Guaraco was the best looking of the lot, with big, sparkling brown eyes that seemed to flash kindness. Her shyness made her instantly likeable. Lithe and nimble, she walked with grace and poise, her every movement seeming to stand out distinctively and make those around her appear to slouch. She was generous to a fault and smiled so often it seemed to her family that she was their own source of cheerfulness.

Pilar was shopping in the local vegetable market one day when a gentleman, who looked to her like a rich American, asked her if she would be interested in a job. He spoke in Spanish and English in quick succession, uncertain of her nationality. She answered right back, flawlessly in both languages, saying the man should ask the question of her father.

Delighted, the man said, "I would be happy to speak to your father. My name is Benjamin Brand. What is your name, young lady?"

"Pilar, sir."

Talk to her father he did, changing the course of her life permanently. To begin work, Pilar was introduced to a man named Omar, a big man, also American. He didn't act especially friendly, although he had kind eyes and a smile that looked a little sad.

Omar told Pilar that she would be a caretaker for a very special guest. For security reasons that were not fully explained, she would never see this guest in person, although he would be able to see her. She could speak to him through a speaker system in the door panel, and meals would be served on a two-way shelf. Her job was to sit by and make herself available if the guest needed anything. That Omar said this was a highly secretive matter of national security did not strike Pilar as troubling. Her country had always had its share of political turmoil, so national security would have to be important. Besides, this job paid nearly four times what similar work paid anywhere else in the country.

She was given a tour of the guest's living area and told she would clean the rooms each day when the occupant had retired to his sleeping quarters. She would deliver his meals on schedule and would be allowed to talk to the guest only if he spoke first.

The guest's rooms were unlike anything she had ever seen. The chairs and tables were huge and mostly made of steel with plush coverings. Tall bookshelves lined most of the walls with what must have amounted to thousands of volumes. Computers with giant screens and an oversized keyboard occupied the far corner. One enormous wall consisted of Interface screens. Pilar knew about these and had seen them before, although her family's rental home still had old-fashioned walls.

On her first day, Pilar arrived just in time to serve the breakfast that arrived from a local food service. Astonished by the number of dishes, she lifted the covers to peek underneath. Never had she seen so much food intended for one person. There must have been a dozen scrambled eggs, at least a dozen pieces of toast, and a bowlful of fresh peaches. A second large bowl bore an engraved import stamp identifying the contents as bindweed salad. Small sticks of bamboo were arranged in a side platter. Puzzled, she placed the dishes on the service door as she had been instructed.

A voice so deep, forceful, and powerful that it sounded as if it had been spoken in a movie theater with the speakers turned up said, "Thank you."

Pilar jumped backwards and nearly fell. After a few moments, she replied in a weak but thoughtful tone, "Thank you, sir."

•◆•

Dark glass prevented anyone from seeing into the room, but from the inside, the view to the outside was crystal clear. The occupant watched the young girl intently, as she darted like a hummingbird, effortlessly moving from one flower to the next. Even when she was doing the simplest things, like preparing to place his food trays in the door, she was mesmerizing to watch. As soon as it was clear to him that his voice frightened her, he made it a point to modify the tone, and he adjusted the volume of the speaker system to soften his voice. He would try to put her at ease.

"What is your name, miss?"

"Pilar, sir."

"Pilar, please do not be afraid. You may call me BenZ, and I promise that you have nothing to fear from me."

"Thank you, sir."

"No need to call me *sir*, either, Pilar. Please sit down and let's get better acquainted."

There was a large chair next to the service door, so she sat down, folded her hands in her lap, and waited for the looming voice to speak again. "Tell me about your family, Pilar."

For the next half-hour, she spoke of her parents and brothers and sisters, the small cottage they rented, and their struggle to survive in a village where there was so much poverty. Every time she stopped talking, BenZ asked another leading question.

Captivated by her presence, he felt a longing, heretofore unknown to him, to reach out and gently touch and caress her. By the time he had spent the whole day with Pilar over breakfast, lunch, and dinner, he was smitten. The very image of the young girl seemed to melt in his mind and then resurface and dissolve in pleasurable feelings, feelings that up to this moment he had never experienced.

After a week passed, BenZ could barely sleep for thinking of Pilar and anticipating the chance to see her again the next morning. Throughout the next month, he and the girl spent time every day talking about every subject imaginable. He began to teach her things, anything she was interested in learning. She was astounded at the depth and breadth of his knowledge. The subject didn't seem to matter. There was nothing that she had mentioned so far that he could not lecture about. No longer afraid of his voice, she was always eager to hear him speak.

One morning, Pilar felt ill and used her communication device to tell her employer that she needed to stay home. Upon seeing a stranger place his food tray through the door, the commanding voice was panic-stricken. Loud noises were heard as several employees were called into the compound. A half-hour later, a staff car brought Pilar by just to say hello. By the time she returned home, an attorney had visited to give her father the deed to the house where they lived. The Guaracos were now owners, not renters. Before he left, the attorney said he wanted to arrange for a construction crew to turn the walls in their home into Interface screens. Pilar's family was ecstatic.

The Eye of the Storm

Three months before Seth sought refuge in the sustainable shelter unit, he had followed a story with great news potential. It began innocently enough, if one could make any claim about the most infamous group of terrorists in the world ever involving innocence. Seth had allowed himself to be blindfolded and driven on the backroads near the Pakistani border to interview Ali Mohema, the current leader of Sephtis.

The two-hour car ride with a human driver seemed to go in circles but finally ended with Seth being led into what felt like a nice home. When his blindfold was removed, he was taken aback and had to fight a sense of panic. Thinking he should forget the interview and run for his life, he quickly came to realize that if he were to run, he would be dead in seconds. Five men were standing almost close enough to touch him, each with knives commonly used for decapitation. They pushed him backward to make room for someone. It was Ali, dressed head-to-toe in black with a blood-red bandana covering his forehead.

"Ali, my name is Seth." The words were barely out of his mouth when a man standing near him slapped him so hard across his face that he almost fell.

An interpreter standing behind Ali, spoke in what sounded like a cross between British and a South African accent, "Speak when you are spoken to and not before. Understood?"

Seth nodded, tasting blood in his mouth, and for the moment he avoided anything more than split-second eye contact with any of the men present. This was a bad idea, a very bad idea. He had known it from the beginning. It was a chance to make big news, but it wasn't worth dying for.

There followed a long moment of silence, and just about the time when Seth thought one of the long knives might take his head, Ali stepped in front of him and said, "Infidels are always without good manners. But you will show respect here or we will not show you the respect of letting you live. Do you understand?"

"Yes, I do." Seth waited so long he began to fear the silence. Despite being told not to speak, he took a chance. "May I begin the interview?"

"You may begin."

Seth asked a dozen carefully crafted questions, editing some in mid-sentence so as not to cross the line of disrespect. The interview went well, considering Seth didn't uncover any earth-shattering revelations about Ali's intentions, but ultimately that's not what made the news.

As he was being driven back to where he was picked up, still blindfolded, he began to mutter to himself as if he were alone. He was venting, as he often did to relieve his exasperation, to quell the fear he felt when he thought he was about to be killed. Moments later, on Interface screens worldwide, Seth appeared being driven in the back seat of a car and wearing a blindfold. His words were loud, the volume apparently turned up for effect. At the bottom of the screen, translations appeared in English, Arabic, French, and German as Seth said, "The great Ali is an embarrassment to Islam. He's a coward hiding behind men with long knives, too fearful to go anywhere without bodyguards. He's an effeminate bastard."

Seconds after his last word, the blindfold was pulled off. He was free to go. The driver had been listening to loud music. The person in the back seat with him had filmed Seth's commentary and uploaded it. In less than a minute, it had gone viral. The only reason Seth was still alive was that his Somali escort and driver could not speak English or Arabic. The driver seemed so absorbed in whatever he was listening to that he was oblivious to what was going on around him, especially since the important part of his task was over. Too bad, because letting Seth go after what he had just said could result in the driver's own decapitation for inattention. The punishment would serve as a chilling warning to Sephtis enemies via Interface news.

Moments after Seth was picked up by JD, he was awash with incoming mail expressing alarm for his safety. He made himself an airline reservation for a flight to New York via AMS airlines, and JD did so separately. They would stay hidden until time for departure.

Before daylight the next morning, Seth and JD headed for the airport. On the way, they picked up a tail. JD turned off the autodrive and took the wheel, driving in the opposite direction of the airport. They were being followed by a black Mercedes carrying what appeared to be six ominous passengers.

For almost an hour, JD tried to shake the tail without being obvious. Finally, at an intersection, just after they cleared a green light that turned yellow, a crowd of people entered the street, enabling him to get far enough ahead so the other car couldn't follow. Ten minutes later, JD said, "Well, we lost the sons of bitches, Seth, but we're going to miss our flight."

•◆•

The Interface evening news worldwide led with an announcement that AMS flight 1419 had crashed minutes after takeoff from the Abudomia airport in Pakistan. The Boeing 797 was carrying 403 passengers. Seth and JD heard the news in hiding, while awaiting their rescheduled flight, the same flight renamed 1519 the next day. Seth's reaction was immediate. "Do you think?"

"Yes, that's what I think," JD said without hesitation. "Had to be."

"But how, how could they know and react that fast? Killing 403 people just to get me. I'm not sure they know about you, or at least that you are with me. It could just be a coincidence."

"Look, until a better explanation comes along, we have to go with it, Seth. As of now, they must think you are dead, but if they find out different and that we are still here, we will be dead soon. Both of us."

The next morning, Seth and JD boarded another 797 and arrived in New York without incident. Seth then flew to Alaska to stay in the community of Palmer, where he had grown up, while JD went to his home in Nashville. Two weeks later, it was announced that the 797 that crashed had bird feathers in both engines. Weeks passed, and Seth got a ping that an encrypted message awaited him. When he was alone and near a receptor screen, he thought, "Read."

EncrypJD: Seth, the feathers and bird DNA from the crash were from domestic ducks. It means both engines were hit with hard metal drones packed with bird matter. It was you they were after, Seth. So far, nothing I've heard indicates they're aware of my being connected to you, but I'm betting they know by now. They just know too much already, and I haven't figured out the leak. You need to hide and lie low for a long time. I'm headed to South America to follow up on a tip that sounds intriguing. I will be in touch soon. Take care and cover, Seth. JD.

Educating Pilar

The weeks turned into months, a year, then the beginning of another. Never during this time had Pilar laid eyes on BenZ, the source of voice that had at first been frightening but now served as an anchor of security and all that was right with the world. Pilar's employers had originally been reluctant to have her spend so much time just talking and listening to her charge, but now they encouraged it, even to the point of hiring another person to do most of the work.

It was also clear that BenZ was educating Pilar in the same manner as a college professor would teach a class of freshmen, but an astute observer would also recognize that these lessons were just as useful to BenZ in putting his own learned views into perspective. He was indeed teaching a student, but most of the time, he was hearing himself make statements that he didn't know he knew until he heard himself make them. To BenZ, Pilar meant clarity, hope, and love.

Early on, at her employer's suggestion, Pilar began to take notes of their discussions, and now she had volumes of notebooks filled with what amounted to a history of civilization. In a deep voice that seemed tempered just for her ears, BenZ explained how the world came to be, how evolutionary biology turned a soup of chemicals into life forms. Those forms mutated, and species emerged only to become extinct in massive die-offs. Finally, man came to be man, and now man's existence was threatening the lives of all the earth's creatures.

At first, Pilar just sat and listened, but as time passed, she began to ask occasional questions. Now she would frequently engage in a dialog that started with a whole line of queries. She was always astounded that, no matter what she asked or how difficult her questions appeared to be, there were always answers that seemed so correct in their logic that they must be true. It was hard to imagine that anyone, anywhere in the world, could know so much.

Sometimes she would go to a village coffee shop frequented by students attending virtual college. Slowly but surely, she was getting over her shyness, and increasingly she found herself sitting at one of the big tables in conversation with the students. To her surprise, she soon realized that she was as well-educated as anyone at the table, even though she had never spent a day in any kind of college environment. Everything she knew she had learned from BenZ.

•◆•

Pilar's family was truly amazed at their good fortune in suddenly being well-off by village standards, with no more worries about finding rent money to keep a roof over their heads. Their previous landlord had tried to get them to pay some additional fees to finalize the sale, but after Pilar mentioned it to BenZ, the landlord had a visitor and soon told Mr. Guaraco that the assessment had been a mistake. Nothing more was due.

At times Pilar's family found the changes in her behavior to be disturbing. Having always been quiet and shy, she was now growing more and more confident and so incredibly articulate that they often had difficulty understanding her. Her employer had fitted her with a state-of-the-art implant, allowing her to engage in Interface forums. That she spoke like an Interface pundit was worrisome.

At night, she often dreamed about her conversations with BenZ, and she fantasied about eloping with him and traveling to America. The portrait she imagined of him in her mind became clearer and clearer, and she began to scheme about how she might get past the security system to see him for herself. With that voice, she thought, he must look like a movie star.

In the evening, and sometimes late at night after her family was asleep, Pilar would join university salons with students signed in from all over the world. She spoke perfect English, but other participants would occasionally assume an air of superiority because of her accent. The first few times she sensed their condescension, she stopped talking and just listened. When she told BenZ about her experiences, he urged her not to accept such treatment, to be proud of who she was, and to speak up.

Taking his advice, she became more aggressive in each session that followed. Finally, a scholarly gentleman suggested one day that she start a forum of her own and lead the discussions. Once she began, her confidence soared, and she recorded her sessions to share with BenZ.

A Strong Objection

For more than two decades, the only news abroad about Benjamin Brand had been from his assistants as they consulted scientists all over the world about DNA properties, genetics, and cloning methodology. Rumors had spread about miraculous scientific breakthroughs from time to time, but rumors were all they ever seemed to amount to. That is, until David Cruz showed up on Capitol Hill in June of 2043. He had information that he said would rock the world of science. But before making the announcement public, he first asked for meetings with members of all branches of the government in private, closed-door sessions.

It was only after CIA director Marvin Winthrop contacted President Oliva Bentley that the idea of a closed congressional committee meeting was proposed. Winthrop explained the content of the message to the president and remarked that the world would never be the same after the meeting. Her reaction to the news caused him to suddenly worry about his future in government. In all his time in dealing with the president, he had never seen her so upset. She raged on and on until he felt he needed to find an excuse to leave. Once outside the White House, he called his deputy and ordered an emergency staff meeting.

Thwarted, David Cruz returned to Peru. When he arrived, he could only report that further negotiations would be necessary before Brand's extraordinary creation could be revealed. To everyone's shock, David died of a heart attack shortly thereafter, leaving Brand and company devastated.

WWBS

he ads were everywhere. Seth figured the Interface payout for *What Would Benzeerilla Say?* must be in the tens of millions of dollars. The problem was that it made no sense. First off, who in the hell was Benzeerilla, and why would anyone care what he, she, or it had to say about anything? JD said there was more to come, but so far, there had been no new messages. He must have used a more obscure encryption service than usual, which meant there would be no way to tell when to expect them to arrive or in what order or format.

Seth would just have to be patient. In the meantime, he asked Amy for an Interface profile of the ad campaign to see if there might be a hint of what the whole thing was about. Just then, he received a message from JD.

JDaEncryp

From JD: Seth, two big notions here, one from the CIA per my intel. The spooks claim Benjamin Brand is planning a terrorist plot on a scale bigger than 42 years ago on 9/11. But informants tell me it's just a ruse to get even with him for doing something horrendous, something for which there's no comparison, something immoral like a cancer on human morality. I have a meeting with someone later today who is supposed to fill in the details. Can't wait. More messages to follow, but for security reasons, you may not receive them in the order I send them. JD.

Abduction

W hen Pilar first began working at the compound, a driverless car was sent each morning to pick her up. Then, after a few weeks, some hushed discussions took place in the control office. Now a driver always sat behind the wheel, both coming and going. He just sat there without driving the vehicle and seldom ever spoke, but Pilar could tell he was armed. The man seemed exceptionally alert, as if searching for something or someone.

One July morning, her car arrived with no driver. The door opened for Pilar to get in, but before she could move, a very large man grabbed her and held her in the air as he ran to a parked vehicle. A door swung open, and the man threw Pilar in like a package with unbreakable contents. She hit her head on the shoulder of another big man in the back seat, and before she could catch her breath to look around, the car sped off, spewing gravel in its wake.

Terrified, Pilar didn't know what to say or what questions to ask. The car windows were darkened to prevent anyone on the outside from seeing the interior clearly. Four armed men were in the car with her, but none of them looked at her. They all focused straight ahead with stern, determined expressions. If she dared to ask them why they had taken her, she knew she would get no answer.

After what seemed like less than half an hour, they stopped at a gate on a narrow road into heavily forested jungle. One of the men got out, opened the gate to let the car through, and locked it behind him. Then they were off again, this time very slowly. The vegetation was so thick and the trees so tall that the air was as dark as dusk. After a few minutes of driving over a rough road, they arrived at a series of Quonset huts. Without speaking, the men got out and the one who had snatched Pilar off the street pulled her towards him. Carrying her with one arm as if packing a lunch, he entered one of the buildings and placed Pilar in a cage with steel bars. Inside were a well-used couch and side chair where Pilar was supposed to sit.

The man had tattoos of ship anchors on both sides of his neck. Glancing around to see if anyone might be watching, he reached down to fondle Pilar's breasts. Horrified, she jerked away in disgust. He stood up, glared at her with a sneering grin, locked the cage, and left without saying a word. It was clear he could do as he pleased with her when he came back.

There were no Interface panels near the cage. Although Pilar had never tried to communicate using her implant alone, she thought there must be a way. She had been unable to see where the driver was taking her. All she knew was that she wasn't very far from home. Still, it was a place she had never been, and she had no idea how to tell anyone where she was. Surely, though, somebody could locate her GPS signal. The kidnappers were not likely to suspect a servant girl of having a sophisticated communication implant.

• ◆ •

An hour after Pilar failed to show up at the compound and the car sent for her had returned without an occupant, a chorus of concern could be heard in the control office and low-octave waves of grief and rage sounded from BenZ's quarters. The compound day manager confirmed to all that a sky camera had recorded Pilar being kidnapped. The bodyguard sent to ride with her had been found and taken to a local clinic to be treated for head trauma.

Five men and three women were in the control room, all of them highly agitated and perplexed about what to do. The noise and confusion went on until just after dark, when loud noises issued from BenZ's quarters, followed by flashing lights and sirens. For the first time ever, BenZ had escaped the compound.

Minutes later, a caravan of vehicles left the facility, two with red lights flashing but no sirens blaring. There was nothing indecisive about their direction. They seemed to know exactly where they were headed, but they weren't speeding. At the same time, in the village, several residents thought they were witnessing the supernatural, as a giant image moved swiftly among the modest homes and through the alleyways, in rhythm with the wind and the flutter of tree leaves. It was as if the spirit of the ancient Incas had once again come alive.

Well before midnight, the creature making the shadows reached a locked gate to an enclosure within the Amazon Jungle. For him, jumping over would have been an effortless feat, but instead, in one fell swoop, he ripped the gate off its hinges and sent it sailing through the air like an errant missile.

Through pitch-black darkness, the shadow-maker moved steadily down the path without a sound. The burly man seated in front of a hut jumped to his feet when he sensed something coming towards him, though he couldn't see anything clearly. In a split second, the darkness before him was blotted out by a presence so large that he didn't know where to look to make sense of it. He reached for the gun holstered at his side, and as he pointed the weapon toward whatever was in from of him, he felt the gun fly from his hand. In the next moment, his arm was wrenched from the shoulder socket, and before he could scream, his head was crushed with a blow that fractured his skull like a lightbulb thrown against a concrete wall.

Another man ran from the back of the building to see what the commotion was, and just as he rounded the corner, he was hit with a one-armed body flying with what seemed like enough G-force to leave the earth's orbit. A light flashed on, and all he saw before losing consciousness was a boat anchor on the neck of the body whose impact broke his back.

Seconds later, the door to the hut was airborne. The noise it made separating from the hinges was like a muffled gunshot. Part of the door facing ripped out at the top as the shadow bent down and entered the building. Inside, he found Pilar in a large cage, hiding under a blanket on a couch. The sound of people running stopped abruptly, and two men with guns drawn stepped carefully into the hut. Before either man could tell what was going on, both died by a single blow from the swat of a giant hand.

Pilar cried out at the sound of the cage door ripping apart. When the blanket was pulled from her and she saw the figure before her, she screamed. Just then, a team of people from Brand's compound dashed into the hut.

BenZ said, "Pilar, it's me, BenZ. Please don't be afraid. You are safe."

Pilar covered her mouth and screamed louder and louder until her voice strained and she fell to the floor. The shadow turned and exited the hut, followed by several men, while two people stayed behind to help Pilar.

Surveillance

J D finished uploading a series of encrypted messages to Seth and turned out the lights in his rented room. Sitting near a window, he looked out through a crack in the blinds. No movement, no lights. The security detector in his pocket showed no activity, but he couldn't shake the feeling that he was being watched. They were out there somewhere, he just knew it. If he sat here in the dark for half an hour, maybe they would figure he had gone to bed.

While he waited, he kept going over what he had learned so far. Benjamin Brand had supposedly created a genetic monster at the fifteen-acre compound near the headwaters of the Amazon that was only about eight miles from his current location. JD had been by the place numerous times.

Brand's compound looked like a CIA high-security head-quarters with a series of electric fences twenty feet tall. Ten inches inside the first fence was another and then another, making it virtually impossible for anyone to climb over. An eighth of a mile was as close as you could get to the compound without going through a gate manned by heavily armed security guards.

JDbEncryp

From JD: Seth, second mindbender coming your way. Have had meetings in Peru near the Amazon. I'm short on absolute proof, but I'm convinced my source believes what he is telling me. I have no doubts about that. You remember that billionaire genius Benjamin Brand relocated to South America decades ago. The claim is that he's created a monster, a creature with human, ape, and chimpanzee DNA, a giant with off-the-charts intelligence and the strength of twenty men. I know it sounds over the top, but the more I hear, the more I believe there is something to it. I keep trying to get a photo as proof, but my source says it is out of the question. This is why I still have some doubts. If the story is true, getting a photo should not be that hard. And if it is true, this will be the story of the century. If we play our cards right, we may have an exclusive. More later. JD.

My Father Who

"You are my father. I have always called you Father, but did it ever occur to you that someday I would wonder about my other two fathers? I presume they live in a zoo, since both species no longer thrive in the wild."

"BenZ, you are the most special living being that has ever existed in the world. You must be aware of how special you are."

"Special? If I have the strength of many men, did you not think that I would have the needs of many? My mother was a lab cocktail, created by you. I am so special that there are no creatures on this planet with whom I am compatible as a mate."

"But BenZ, we have been over this before. You will soon have a mate."

"Are you not aware that I despise my own likeness and that I care for a person, a human, a young girl who is horrified by the very sight of me?"

"Yes, and I'm very sorry about that."

"I want you to terminate the process."

"BenZ, please, you need company."

"Do it or I will do it for you. What difference will another failed experiment make? We are only about thirty yards from the graveyard of what we might call my cousins, or maybe brothers and sisters. You know, the ones who weren't quite ready, as I'm guessing you probably put it?"

"BenZ, please. Are you not glad to be alive? I created you, in effect, to help save the world by holding up a mirror to mankind, by having you tell us what we cannot see for ourselves. All these years that you've spent studying Eastern and Western culture have been preparation so that you can be one of the most important entities who has ever lived. BenZ, you can have importance in the history of man on a platform as exalted as Christ, the Buddha, or Muhammad."

"You mean *you* will have such a place in history, not me. I will not even be considered a *me*. Or an *I*. The entity that should be me is but a freak. History is simply a shorthand record of those with money and power. You will be forever infamous for having created a twenty-first-century Frankenstein. That's what you mean, don't you, Father? I am but an expression of your pride. Deny it if you must, but do not expect me to believe it, because I know it's not true. Truth is what I'm supposed to be about, is it not, Father?"

"BenZ, please. What I'm doing is not for me and me alone—that's just not my intention. I have never in my life fit in the social culture I was born into. I've been odd man out from the beginning—as a child, a teenager, and now as an aging adult. You and I have that much in common. The only way I can justify my existence for having been gifted with my own level of intelligence is to contribute in the only way I know how, and that is with you and what you are going to bring to the world, what you are going to enable people to see. You have the perspective and complete objectivity of a superior entity far more intelligent than homo sapiens."

"And if I refuse, Father?"

"Please, BenZ. We have been hard at work on this project for years. We are close, so very close. I'm going back to America soon to arrange things. I want you to stay here in the jungle compound until I get back. Then I will take you to America."

"I want to see my other two fathers before I leave."

"BenZ, please."

"I insist."

"Let me consider it."

"You must do more than consider it because, if you do not arrange it, I will not go to North America."

In Hiding

The safe house where Pilar was temporarily staying had only
two windows, one in front and one in back. She would sit
near one for a while and then move to the other. Shame and
embarrassment consumed her because of the way she had acted
at the first sight of her mentor. All those days spent dreaming
were shattered in a split second when she saw what she had never
come close to suspecting. It was irresponsibly naïve of her not to
have assumed there were good reasons why she had never been
allowed to see the person whose imagined visage she had grown
to love, the one she dreamed of day and night and hoped to share
her life with always.

Now all of that was gone, and now, having spent hour after
hour reflecting about the whole experience, she couldn't help but
think how hurt BenZ must have been when she screamed like a
schoolgirl watching a horror movie. No apology could ever take
that away. Would it even be possible to resume their relationship
as teacher and student again, or even as friends? She kept visu-
alizing another possible meeting in her mind, and it never felt
comfortable, no matter what she imagined that she or he said.
Even when she slept, she dreamed of hearing that deep but tender

and affectionate voice that she had grown so fond of. But now, knowing from whom that voice came, she wondered if things could ever be anywhere close to the same as before.

For the first two days, she had cried constantly. Now she just felt sad and didn't want to see anyone or talk to anyone about anything. The three armed guards protecting her made every attempt to be friendly and helpful. Pilar appreciated this, but it added to her anxiety because she didn't want to hurt their feelings.

When she was told she would be taken to a safe house, the woman named Ms. Tyson had explained to Pilar that guards had been sent to her home to protect her family. As soon as the situation was thoroughly assessed and fully understood by security, she would be allowed to leave. At the very least, they hoped to send her home next week, and she was not to worry about her job, as she had been through a horrible ordeal. She would remain on the payroll and would be called to come back to work once some issues in America were resolved. In the meantime, a security detail would keep watch on her and her family.

Ms. Tyson said nothing about BenZ, and Pilar had been too embarrassed to ask. Now she was sorry she hadn't inquired, and this added to her worry. She had no idea how to get a message to him unless the guards were somehow able to help. There were no Interface screens in the house, presumably for security reasons, but she longed for distraction, something to get her mind off the fact that her world, her life, and her hopes and aspirations would likely never be as before.

Alone

Imagining a future without JD was unbearable. Seth had slept
on and off for days with dreamlike remembrances of the two
of them in their glory days when they were the big thing in
Interface news. He knew that he should get serious about how
to proceed and take some action, but depression won out. The
malady had bothered him all his life, and at times like now, the
bouts could be overwhelming. The shelter system offered the
most reliable civilian security in the country. If he stayed inside
his unit, he would be safe, but he would be letting the bullies win.

Maybe he should leave Alaska now and go to Tennessee to
visit JD's family. He had met JD many years before in Nashville,
and Tennessee was where he had a business project underway
that he had placed in the hands of two nieces and a nephew. The
place was nearly ready to open. It involved the kind of work he
had always intended to do. Of course, his life there would likely
be less exciting, but if he was right, the business would provide a
good living for him and his kin. The setting was a beautiful place
for reflection.

Years earlier, he had purchased 120 acres in a heavily wooded
area just off the interstate in Tennessee and had staked his family

members for putting his plan to work. They carefully cleared part of the land, enough for a winding road among tall timber that would allow visitors to drive through the property. The attraction would be the first-ever Kudzu Zoo. Seth had designed steel frames in the shapes of dinosaurs and all sorts of prehistoric creatures with the notion of having the fast-growing kudzu planted within the frames to fill them out. The sight of the plant-like creatures would draw tourists off the interstate for a drive among giant visual treats, with shops along the way for food and souvenirs.

Three investment firms had laughed at his business plan before he found one that was wildly enthusiastic. Most recently, his niece and project manager had reported that they would be ready to open as soon as the plants had fully grown into their frames. Judging from the rate the kudzu was growing, the park should be able to open this fall.

Before Seth could become involved, though, he would have to declare himself back in business. Doing that would mean he would have to give up the security of the shelter. It was a very troubling move. Perhaps now he would never be free enough to again live in the open. All because he had let off some emotional angst that no one should have heard. How could he have been so stupid? Even if the driver couldn't speak English, wouldn't he have had an implant that could interpret? He knew that was unlikely, but it didn't help now.

Why hadn't he insisted that JD take shelter as he had? But then, JD was still traveling and working, so it wasn't an option. He'd promised JD that he would someday have him help run the Kudzu Zoo in a manner that would resemble a kind of retirement. Now, just thinking about the project made him feel ill. Now, no matter in what context he tried to frame the past, it was clear to him that, except for his own stupidity, JD would still be alive.

JDcEncryp

Getting hot here, Seth. I'm being followed. Harder than hell to lose them. Something is going on here with the CIA, so it must be them on my tail. My sources confirm the CIA is focused on a young girl named Pilar Guaraco. They think she is a key to their breaching the security of Brand's compound. My informant says the CIA hasn't seen the creature they claim Brand has created, but my best source has told me that, shortly after Oliva Bentley was sworn in as president, she became obsessed with what the agency has been telling her about what's happening down here. No one seems to know much more than that. My guess is that it has something to do with the moral platform that got her elected. She wants to move back to the political hard right, especially when it comes to biotechnology.

Also, I have a contact who claims they can give me the locations of Sephtis in Detroit, Chicago, and the Middle East. I'm sending them a message routed to you. All they must do is provide addresses or coordinates and then the message comes to you automatically. They don't have to provide the information, but they can't stop it from eventually coming to you. If they don't provide the information in the time allowed, you will get the message anyway, *minus the locations. But you won't get it unless they have received it first. If you don't hear anything at all, it just means they weren't legit. Gotta go. Stay safe. JD.*

Trapped

JD waited until he got the secret hand signal that meant this was the person he was supposed to meet. He didn't think he was being followed this time, but he could never be sure that drones weren't tracking his every move, high enough and sky-camouflaged to make them almost impossible to spot. Although he had waited until dark, the drones could photograph in infrared, so all he could do was hope he wasn't in someone's crosshairs. Entering a shack that looked as if it might collapse in a light breeze, he saw a small man motioning for him to sit down on a wobbly bench. JD took a deep breath and said, "Do you have pictures?"

"No way, mister. I told you, no one can get that close."

"Then how do I know what you have been telling me is true?"

"All I can do is tell you what I've been told, and I have every reason to believe my source."

"Then tell me who your source is."

"That I can't do. I can't do it without putting someone's future in real jeopardy. I know my story sounds bizarre, but if what I've been telling you isn't true, why do you think you've been followed so many times?"

"Look, there are all sorts of reasons why I might be under surveillance, but what you have told me till now is completely off the charts. I need some kind of proof."

"I've pleaded with my source for pictures, but was told that if I mention it again, they will stop giving me information."

"So, if you have nothing new, then why did you ask to meet?"

"I do have something, something very important I think. The pretty young girl I told you about, the one who sits all day and carries on conversations with the creature? She was kidnapped by some hired goons. They took her down river about three or four miles and locked her in a cage. The creature became upset, tracked her down in darkness, flew into a rage, and literally butchered some of the bastards who were guarding the girl. Tore them limb from limb, he did. When the girl saw the creature for the first time, she freaked out. Now they've taken the creature away, and my source is not exactly sure where or why."

"And how do you know this?"

"My source was present when they found the girl and brought her back home. Now the people who hired the goons are fuming. That's all I know."

After the older man left, JD stayed on the bench, composing messages to Seth. A half-hour later, he walked outside. In the next instant, he lost consciousness, unable to see who had just hit the back of his head with what felt like a baseball bat.

Father's Day

Special arrangements were made for a motorcade with an enormous motor home to enter the zoo after closing hours under cover of darkness. It had taken some very persuasive conversations and ultimately a substantial contribution to the zoo to make this visit possible. The hardest thing to sell the zoo officials was the need for secrecy and total assurance that the two primates involved would not be physically harmed or involved in any kind of biological experiment. It had been a difficult negotiation, and Mr. Brand's instructions had been that under no circumstances was she to give up until the deal was firm. So, Samantha Tyson persevered, made the arrangements, and now, as agreed, would wait outside as her passenger entered the zoo.

Serving as Benjamin Brand's compound and laboratory supervisor was a very taxing but satisfying experience for Samantha. Still, she worried that, under the right circumstances, her whole life's work could implode overnight, reputation ruined. For years, she had focused so narrowly on her charge that she had stopped thinking about the big-picture question of morality that went hand-in-glove with such a risky experiment. Brand's employee since graduate school, she was also his lover, but they had never married, a fact that tormented her when she thought about growing old and remaining single. Her stake in Brand International, Inc., was of untold value, and she would likely have to carry her deepest-held secret with her to her grave. The full realization of this was beginning to gnaw at her conscience.

Inside the zoo lay an old, graying chimpanzee named Brutus, who had once been an alpha-male and ruler of his laboratory compound when he was not caged by himself. Now, nearly fifty and dying, he was so feeble, he could barely sit upright. He would already have been euthanized had it not been for the arrangement with Brand International to have him available for a special visitor.

The light was dim, and the visitor who entered cast a shadow so large it made the room go dark. The visitor knelt as Brutus looked up, his face taut, his sad eyes barely open. A huge hand slipped under his head and neck, slowly lifting him into a sitting position. For the next hour, no sounds were made, only slight gestures, with eyes locked in an embrace of mutual understanding. The old chimpanzee blinked and at times seemed intently alert, and then his eyes would close and he would appear to sleep, only to open his eyes wide again as if he were only now awake. Finally, he shut his eyes one last time, and his breathing stopped. The visitor lay Brutus back down, caressed him gently for a moment, and then went down a corridor to another large cage with steel bars, opened the gate, and entered.

Sitting in the corner was Terry, or Terrible Terry, as he was referred to by the zoo staff. He was an ill-tempered, aging silverback mountain gorilla, one of the last of his kind. The only remaining members of his species lived in captivity. Terry jumped to his feet when the visitor began to approach. He made a roaring sound, beating his chest in a staccato tempo. Screaming, he stepped forward with arms in the air ready to strike the visitor.

Suddenly, both of his arms were seized, and he was powerless to move.

Terry made eye contact with the visitor, who made some grunting noises and after a few minutes let Terry's arms go free. He started to strike again but stopped, and the visitor took a seat where Terry had been sitting and looked at him as if pleading for something. Terry sat down beside him, and the visitor made more grunting sounds. Even though the visitor towered over Terry, the aging silverback sensed no threat. The visitor put his arms around Terry and pulled him close.

For nearly two hours, they sat together making eye contact and occasionally breaking the silence with grunts and whimpering gestures. Had any of the zookeepers been present, they would have claimed that what was occurring was simply not possible. They would have said Terrible Terry would have fought to the death rather than be touched as he had.

An hour before daylight, the caravan of vehicles left the zoo. Four days later, just for the sake of public relations, Samantha called the zoo director, who told her the staff had found that Brutus had died during the visit and that Terry had been unusually subdued ever since. He wanted further assurance that Terry had not been drugged and that Brutus had not been killed. Samantha told the director that Brutus had died in the arms of his visitor and was at peace. The silence on the other end of the phone went on so long that Samantha thought the director had hung up. Finally, the director said, "Okay."

Conspiracy

At age 57, Benjamin Brand looked 70. His hair was white, his face drawn and tense. There were no noticeable wrinkles, and yet his features appeared frozen serious. He seemed troubled, like someone engaged in a life-threatening venture and unsure how it would turn out. Today he wondered if he might be making a mistake. His jet was on approach to a large but private airport near Atlanta. He had not been back in the United States for decades.

The pilot made a perfectly smooth landing, as was expected by his employer. The aircraft taxied to a stop near a large hanger, and as soon as Benjamin exited and placed both feet on the ground, a cadre of vehicles appeared out of nowhere. They slammed to a stop as if choreographed to do so, and a dozen men in dark suits surrounded Benjamin and his pilot and assistants.

A short, bald agent with broad shoulders thrust a badge high in the air as if grudgingly meeting a minimum procedural requirement. Without hesitation, the man said, "Mr. Brand, you are under arrest for sedition."

Two minutes later, an empty aircraft with its doors still open sat abandoned with no one in sight. Interface bulletins flashed, "Billionaire Benjamin Brand arrested on suspicion of treason and terrorism."

Broken

J D felt excruciating pain in his arms and shoulders. His hands tied behind him had lost all feeling as the flow of blood stopped. Through blurred vision, he was slowly regaining consciousness. His attempts at becoming lucid were like a flock of starlings in flight, fluttering about and unsure where to land. Suddenly someone was standing close, and when JD tried to focus, his head jerked to one side from a hard slap by an open hand.

"Wake up, infidel. Wake up, or I will put you back to sleep permanently." The man standing before him was white and his accent was American, but he was wearing the garb of Sephtis. Obviously, he was a sympathizer recruited via Interface.

Trying hard to awaken fully, JD said, "Where am I? What do you want of me?" As he spoke, he realized the man was not wearing a mask, which could only mean one thing: If this man didn't care that JD could recognize him, then his willingness or unwillingness to cooperate was meaningless. He was already a dead man.

"You are in Ecuador. You know what I want. Did you forget so easily? We want the location of Seth Shepard. We know he is in Alaska, but not precisely where, and that is what you are going to tell me. You understand?"

"No, I'm not. I don't know where he is, and even if I did, I wouldn't tell you." Someone behind him lifted him out of his chair, someone big enough to handle him as effortlessly as a longshoreman hoisting a sack of goods. JD felt his arms fly upwards as he was lifted off the ground. His shoulder sockets began to tear, the pain blinding, so much so that, even though he was being spoken to, he could not make sense of what was being said. Then his world went dark again.

For hours, he would awaken only to lose consciousness moments later. When he managed to stay awake long enough to harbor a thought, it was only to wish for a quick death. He had lost complete track of time. The only thought that gave him comfort was that he had already sent Seth everything he needed to know before being taken hostage.

A hard slap to his head forced open his eyes. Another face was so close to his that he could not see it clearly, but the breath was noxious and horrid. "When I return, each time I ask a question and you refuse to answer, we will cut off a finger. If we run out of fingers, we start on your toes, then your arms and legs. Do you understand?"

Big Trouble Ahead

ENCRYPFROMJD

Hot news, Seth. A jackpot scoop I daresay for sure this time. Two things going on here. First, if the creature Brand has created is as I'm told, then this is surely the biggest thing we will have ever reported on. Benzeerilla is part chimpanzee, part mountain gorilla, and part man. He is enormous in size, with the strength of twenty men and an IQ in the stratosphere. I know all the scuttlebutt focuses on the immorality of what Brand has done, but my impression is that Brand has had noble intentions all along. I know this sounds rather weak, but at this point, I'm pretty much convinced. What I've been told is that Brand has a messianic complex and not only does he believe what he has created is not sacrilegious, he thinks he is doing the world a great humanitarian service by raising a mirror to humans so that we can see ourselves from the perspective of other creatures for the first time. That's the reason for all the What Will Benzeerilla Say advertising. So, it's got me wondering just what the hell this creature can say to make all this worthwhile.

Now, the other thing I have, from a different source, is that Brand's organization has been infiltrated by Sephtis. David Cruz, who was Brand's tutor when he was young and who worked for Brand for the rest of his life, had a couple of nephews by marriage, who are from Pakistan. As a favor to Cruz, Brand employed them, and he must have done so without background checks because these guys are terrorists for sure. My Pakistani informant says they're involved in a major plan of some kind to poison water supplies in the U.S. and Europe. He thinks they also intend to destroy Brand's laboratory, kill the staff, and put the creature on display for the whole world to ridicule.

So, if something should happen to me, you must warn Brand. I'm starting to wonder if maybe the very reason I received these tips about Brand in the first place is because of my connection with you. It's just a hunch at this point, but I can't get the idea out of my mind. You need to get in touch with Brand as soon as possible, but you'll probably have to go in person because he's heavily protected with security and staff. My source from inside the Brand compound is someone who works for a woman named Samantha Tyson, his top associate. Apparently, Tyson is also Brand's lady friend. God, what a story this is turning out to be!

Don't forget, if something happens to me, you must get to Brand. Doing so could save thousands of lives. I'm told the poison these people have developed doesn't show up in a test unless you know what you're testing for. Can you imagine what kind of damage that could do? Sephtis has big money behind it, and these guys are out for blood and humiliation. Of course, we know this as well as anyone, don't we? For you and me to ever walk about carefree again, these guys are going to have to be destroyed. See you soon. JD.

Checkmate

The room was large, the lights bright, and the conference table small. The idea was to make one of the occupants feel diminished, but it wasn't working. Benjamin Brand sat at one end of the table, hands and elbows resting in front of him, as if he were simply relaxing from a day's work. A smartly dressed gentleman entered the room and said, "Mr. Brand, do you know who I am?"

"Yes, I know your name is Marvin, and you're the director of the CIA. Don't recall your last name, though."

"Winthrop."

"Is that important?"

"Perhaps only to me. But, Mr. Brand, I've spent more time with President Bentley in the last few days that I care to. She is consumed with anger over what she thinks you have done. Nevertheless, all we have are rumors. No one in the administration has confirmation. If what we have been led to believe is true, however, I would say you are in deep trouble, sir."

"And what does she think is true? What does she think I have done?"

"Ever since your man David Cruz showed up here a few months ago, she thinks you are the father of blasphemy. That's the way she puts it, or at least that's what she says when she isn't in a rage and cursing like a drunken sailor. So, is it true, Mr. Brand? Are you the face of evil, as she believes?"

"Most assuredly not, Mr. Winthrop."

"Look, we know for certain that you employ members of Sephtis."

"Excuse me?"

"You heard me, Mr. Brand."

"Nonsense."

"Two of your employees are from Pakistan, right?"

"Yes, they are nephews by marriage of David Cruz, who was my friend and employee until he passed away."

"Well, sir, I have two files, each an inch thick, documenting that not only are they Sephtis members, they are also part of a network that's plotting acts of biological terrorism here and abroad. I suppose you're going to tell me that you don't know anything about this, correct?"

"Correct, absolutely correct. If what you say is true, this has happened completely without my knowledge. I gave those young men jobs as a favor to a dear friend. I seldom see or talk to either of them. If you have reliable evidence against them, by all means pick them up and charge them."

"We will, of course, in due time. A couple of our agents seem convinced that you may indeed have been unaware of such things going on in your organization, sir, but even if that turns out to be the case, it still doesn't let you off the hook. My boss, our president, is a moralist. She never lets up on her campaign promise to renew a sense of morality in America, and she has become obsessed with the idea that you are doing the work of the devil—her words, not mine. I don't think she has ever believed that you are a terrorist, but I think the possibility matters less to her than what she suspects you are up to, tinkering with human and animal DNA. Is she right?"

"Whose morality are we talking about, Mr. Winthrop? The morality of the Christian God, who demanded sacrifices and whose worship includes the drinking of metaphoric blood in tribute to a preposterous absurdity? That human beings can believe such nonsense is itself a sign of immorality."

"Look, spare me the lecture. I couldn't care less about the religious implications. I just want to know what is going on. I'll say this, Mr. Brand. You are a man of many resources and I daresay a man of strategy as well. We were all set to stick you with the label of terrorist, send you to a black site, and forget about you. Then the head of the stock exchange pointed out that you are set to trigger a financial earthquake. We knew you were a very rich man, sir, but not that you're so devious, if that's what it is. In any event, you have the president's attention, so how do we proceed? How do we both get what we want without a financial meltdown and a moral crisis of faith in humankind?"

"You can start by cutting me loose. If you don't, there will indeed be consequences."

"I will see what I can do, sir. But you must give me something I can use to calm the president, and it is going to have to be good."

"Turn me loose and I will return home to bring the subject of my work back here with me. We will testify before Congress about the nature of our work and the reasons for it, and the president can judge for herself. I don't mean to be flippant by saying the world needs to hear what Benzeerilla has to say."

Connection

Working by himself was unnerving. Without JD, Seth was losing confidence. A sense of guilt haunted him for not appreciating how much he depended on JD until he was gone. The one thing he did have, though, was access to JD's whistle-blower database, TELLJD. He had never accessed it, but JD always made it clear that if something were to happen to him, Seth should login with JD's credentials, change the password, and continue the administration as if he were JD.

Being unfamiliar with the system, Seth experienced some initial confusion, trying to sort the insane messages by crackpots from the ones that might have merit. Since he had no access to JD's Clyde, he put Amy to work. He was about to give up on finding anything with a worthwhile connection to Benjamin Brand when he saw a brief message that Brand had been released from federal custody and was in Washington, D.C., awaiting further government investigation. Seth asked Amy to begin immediately to find the location of where Benjamin Brand was staying in D.C. He figured there was a good chance that Amy would have the answer by the time he got there.

Now, he just had to figure a way to get to the airport in Anchorage without being attacked by drones or worse. If he was going to be gone longer than two weeks, he would have to check out of his shelter unit. So, he submitted his intention to be on vacation and to return in less than two weeks. If delayed in any way, he would let the manager know.

The ride to Anchorage was mercifully uneventful. The unmanned vehicle Seth ordered already had two passengers, and the trip took less than an hour. He detected no warnings from his security sentinel system, but this was worrisome, since he was sure they knew where he was. That there had been no follow-up attempt on his life was puzzling. All during the drive to the airport, he watched for other vehicles, and even scanned the sky for signs of being followed. The couple who sat facing him kept looking at each other, as if signaling that they knew who they were traveling with and that he was acting a bit strange. Maybe Seth's paranoia was getting the best of him, but he figured it was better to be overly wary than sorry.

It had been three years since he was last in D.C. Amy found him a room less than a mile from where she guessed that Benjamin Brand was staying. Seth was amused when he saw her logic. The day that Brand was released from custody, someone had leased the top floor of the new Roosevelt Hotel. How Amy came to such a conclusion and how she made such discoveries was a mystery, but he figured there was a 75 percent chance she was right. So now, if that was the case, if Brand had leased a whole floor for security reasons, how in the world could he break through and make contact?

He found where JD had sketched a rough organizational chart of Brand International, and it contained a photo of a woman named Samantha Tyson, who appeared to run daily operations. Since he still had his press credentials and at least second- or third-tier access to most of the important people in the Western Hemisphere, he ordered Amy to contact Samantha Tyson with a message subject of life-or-death urgency.

Five hours later, he received an Interface call from Ms. Tyson. "Hello, Seth. Samantha Tyson here. Seeing you now, I realize I've seen you before. I thought your name was familiar but wasn't sure if you were a legit newsman. What do you have to tell me that is so urgent and life-threatening?"

"Thank you for calling, Ms. Tyson. First, do you know for sure that we are visiting on a secure frequency? I know it says we are, but calls like this have been known to be subject to hacking."

"Mr. Brand is fanatical about security, so I assure you we are not being copied."

"Okay, I'll be blunt and come right out with it. My assistant, Justin Davis, went to South America a while back on a tip about what has been going on at Mr. Brand's laboratory near the Amazon River. He was led to believe you folks have created a monster. Ms. Tyson, JD was murdered there. One of the last messages I received from him said there was a plan by the Sephtis group to kill all your personnel and take your creature hostage. They intend to make a world spectacle of him, her, it, or whatever it is you have made, and while they are at it, they intend to pull off some acts of biological terrorism in the U.S. and Europe."

"And where and how did he uncover such a plot?"

"He was a very resourceful investigator. I feel certain someone inside your organization has been feeding him information."

"But, Sephtis? Really, that's preposterous."

"You have some young men on your staff from Pakistan, right?"

A long moment of silence followed. "Can we meet in person, Seth? I would like to introduce you to Benjamin Brand."

•➤•

The two security guards who escorted Seth into the hotel suite looked like people it would be a big mistake to mess with. A very attractive middle-aged woman with auburn hair and penetrating green eyes came forward and said, "Hello, I'm Samantha Tyson. You may call me Sam."

Seth was surprised, stunned really, as the pictures he had seen of her didn't do her justice. She looked decidedly smart and must have once been drop-dead gorgeous. No wonder Brand had latched on to her. "Thank you. Is Mr. Brand here now?"

"He will be with us shortly. Can we get you anything, coffee, tea, a drink maybe? Water?"

Seth could see she was trying hard not to stare at his eyes. "Coffee would be great, black."

Sam spoke to someone via Interface, and in less than a minute, a gentleman wearing a chef's hat entered the room and handed Seth a cup of coffee from a tray. "Can I get you something to eat perhaps?"

"No, thank you," said Seth, adding, "Damned good coffee." The cook smiled, nodded in approval, and left the room.

Just then, Seth detected an emergency vibration. "May I use a screen, please? Really quick?"

"Sure, be my guest."

Seth pulled up an Interface screen that only he could see and asked Amy for help with the incoming encrypted message. It was from JD with information about the locations of Sephtis operating centers. Three spaces with a date appeared that would require that Seth apply his own interpreter to decode the input. His hands began to shake, too unsteady to correctly hit the keys on the keyboard facsimile he was using.

"Are you okay?"

"God, I hope so. This could be the break I need to be free to walk the street again without being paranoid. If I can just calm down for a minute, and if this is what I hope it is, we need to run it up the flag pole."

"What is it?"

"Hopefully it's what JD said might be coming my way—the locations, three to be exact, for Sephtis here and the main head-quarters in Pakistan or Syria." Taking a deep breath, he typed slowly and deliberately. "Got it. Let's show Mr. Brand."

A distinguished-looking gentleman entered the room and nodded at Seth but kept his distance. "Sam told me who you are and what you are up to. You want to give me the gist of it?"

"Yes, sir. I won't waste your time with small talk. I've been a freelance newsman for years. My assistant, or I guess I should say my working partner, was murdered a short time ago near your place in South America. He was butchered. As I told Ms. Tyson, he was working on a tip that you have created something of a Frankenstein monster, but in addition, he learned that you have members of Sephtis in your employ. You and all your employees are now targets for assassination, and your so-called monster is going to be put on display as the work of Satan.

"Also, sir, early this morning I learned that a platoon-strength group of terrorists from Pakistan is on its way to your laboratory. I do not know how they are traveling or when precisely they will arrive, but they are being aided by some of the people who work for you. On top of that, our sources say that Sephtis is also plan-ning some acts of biological terrorism in the U.S. and Europe. Just moments ago, sir, I got the location of Sephtis in this country and in Pakistan."

"How sure are you that the information is good?"

"I just have no reason to doubt it, sir. I trust my source."

"So, what is your plan? What are you going to do with the information you have so far?"

"To go on the air with it, sir."

"Do you have enough contacts to keep getting information as this thing rolls out?"

"I think so. I'm working on my partner's platform and have no reason to think the informants will stop feeding me information, unless they find out that JD is dead."

"Look, young man. You don't have enough information about what I'm doing to do anything but embarrass yourself if you try to report it now. You wait here, though, and keep quiet. In a couple of weeks, I will come back and give you a real story."

"Mr. Brand, I'm also at the top of a Sephtis hit list, with a million-dollar bounty for my life and another million for my head, literally for my head. I'm the reason AMS flight 1419 crashed and all those people were killed. Sephtis was trying to kill me."

"I thought that was a bird strike," said Samantha.

"JD found out those were domestic ducks, but that hasn't been made public."

"Then you should go back to Peru with us," said Brand.

"You mean go where Sephtis is headed?"

"We will keep you safe. I've already asked the CIA to pick up the two young men who work for me at the compound."

"And we can be back in less than two weeks?"

"Yes. Give me the locations for Sephtis, and maybe we can put an end to this nonsense before it begins. I'm in direct contact with the head of the CIA, who can inform the president."

Brand left the room, and a few minutes later, at CIA headquarters, Marvin Winthrop's secretary took Benjamin Brand's call and put it through to the director.

"Hello, Mr. Brand. You aren't changing your mind about the committee meeting, are you?" Marvin said.

"No, but I have something that you might want to take care of right away. It might very well change your mind about pulling something with my guest speaker after the hearing."

"And why do you assume we intend to do that?"

"I didn't get this far, Mr. Winthrop, by being naïve. I've read the president's comments about what she thinks we have done, and I know she would not have agreed to my terms if she didn't have ulterior motives. I'm not wrong, am I?"

Winthrop let his silence be answer enough. "So, what do you propose, sir. What do you have to trade?"

"How about the location of Sephtis headquarters in Pakistan and two strongholds here in the states?"

Oval Office

"**M**adam President, I have given Secretary of Defense Holt the coordinates for two Sephtis strongholds in the U.S., one in Detroit and one in Chicago, and a third that is said to be their main headquarters in Pakistan. I got this information from Benjamin Brand. He already suspects that we have something in mind after the committee hearing. I indicated to him that we would take his concerns into consideration, although I made no promises."

"Good, Marvin, because this doesn't change my mind."

"But, Madam President, if this information is correct, we might be able to catch Sephtis flat-footed and strike a lethal blow very soon."

"I agree, Marvin, but that doesn't excuse the moral blasphemy the Brand group is shoving in our face. Sit down." Then, speaking to a communication device, she said, "Get me Secretary Holt."

"Good evening, Madam President. Or should I say night? It's late."

"Leonard, what do you make of the information Marvin gave you?"

"We've already had a look in Detroit and Chicago. These locations are occupied, but nothing particularly suspicious appears to be going on. Both are vacant as of now. Too early to tell on Pakistan. We will stay on it, Madam President, and will keep you informed."

"Thank you, Len. Just keep them under surveillance for now. There is something I want to take care of first." Turning to face Marvin, she said, "This may turn out to be bogus information. It could be Brand's way of trying to save face. Once we have taken care of his unspeakable behavior, we will eliminate Sephtis."

"Madam President, I assure you Benjamin Brand doesn't think he has done anything wrong. In fact, he thinks he is doing the world a great public service. I recommend we round up these terrorists now before they have a chance to hit us."

Marvin Winthrop had a manner about him like that of a judge who's feared by defense attorneys and sucked up to by prosecutors, but President Bentley was not intimidated. "I'm the one doing the world a public service, here. Let's not forget that. In due time, Marvin. In due time, we will put them behind bars along with Frankenstein."

Venturing South

The Brand corporate jet was state-of-the-art, with Interface screens wherever there was room. Seth was sitting by himself in the rear of the aircraft, trying fitfully to sleep, but he had too much on his mind. Was he making another enormous mistake, just like the one that put a price on his head? Never had he spent so much time questioning his own judgment, but he assured himself he had plenty of cause. He was putting a lot of trust in Benjamin Brand. How could he be sure Brand could keep them safe with a hoard of terrorists coming to kill them? Capturing Seth would just be a bonus. Once again, his mind flashed on a picture of his head being shipped overnight in a FedEx box.

The only thing that convinced him to accompany Brand to Peru was the fact that the CIA was already investigating the existence of Sephtis in his organization and the knowledge that Brand had conveyed to the CIA the information from JD about the new threat headed to his compound. Next in his thoughts was an insatiable curiosity about Brand's project. Why would anyone believe that creating a freak of nature, which most people would think of as blasphemous, could in any way be considered an achievement? The logic escaped him. Maybe if he could spend

some time alone with Sam or Brand, he could be made to understand, but he thought it doubtful.

The upside he was counting on was that, between the CIA
and Brand, and possibly the American and allied military,
Sephtis would be hurt so badly that he could live again in the
open without outright paranoia. If this was indeed the big story
JD thought it was originally, then he would use it to get back on
the air permanently. The only thing that could interfere would be
his lasting remorse about JD.

•◆•

As the jet began its gradual descent, Samantha was wondering if bringing Seth was a mistake. She had known all along that
one day the project would be front-page news the world over, but
now that it could only be weeks away, she feared her reputation
could suffer irreparable damage. Until this stranger showed up
with news of a security breach coming from within their own
ranks, she had not been so worried. Some secrets were too sensitive to ever be made public, their origins better left undiscovered.

The Compound

Just before the jet touched down, Seth glanced out the window. He could see a small village of perhaps a few thousand inhabitants surrounded by Peruvian jungle and what must be the Brand headquarters a half-mile or so in the distance. It was impressive. Enclosed behind high, double and triple fences of barbed wire and electrified wire, it looked more like a military post than a laboratory.

Earlier, while waiting for the aircraft to be fueled, Sam had explained to Seth that Brand was mostly responsible for the village's very existence. In the early years, Brand routinely hired people who stayed close by, and as the years passed, a whole thriving village grew up near the compound. The people in the village were poor by North American standards, but they were not impoverished. Brand's contributions had raised the standard of living above that of many other villages. He had established a clinic in the village years ago, and when medical emergencies occurred that the local doctors couldn't handle, Brand made his aircraft available for public use, turning him into something of a hero.

They were met by a limousine, and minutes later, they arrived at the main gate to the compound. Sam motioned for Seth to walk with her. Upon entering a door that looked like a bank vault, she said, "This is the main building. Our living quarters are in the back. Over here is our guest room and what we call our education facility."

The size of the furniture was almost frightening. That anything would be large enough to require this much space was hard for Seth to imagine. "Are you going to show me whoever makes use of this furniture?" he asked.

"In due course, we will. But our guest is away now. We have another highly secure location deep in the jungle. It's completely inaccessible except by helicopter. Let me show you where you will be staying while we're here. Just follow me."

Seth was shocked to see the amenities in his room. Three times the size of his shelter unit, it included a small kitchen and Interface screens everywhere, providing more than enough space to work. To his surprise, dinner was bought to his room, the food delicious.

As soon as he finished eating, he logged on to JD's site and put Amy to work. Nothing definitive was coming up yet about the terrorist insurgents supposedly on the way to kill them. Just the thought of that was creepy. Alarming information had been received during the flight south that Pilar's kidnappers were indeed connected with Sephtis. At least it had been a relief to learn in addition that local authorities had taken Brand's two employees into custody and were questioning others.

Still troubling, though, was the fact that the two men had been in Brand's organization for a long time, long enough to know an awful lot about Brand's facilities and how things worked. Otherwise, Sephtis wouldn't have had enough confidence to send people here on the assumption that they could successfully carry out such a tall order.

• ◆ •

Early the next morning, Seth received a notice via Amy that botanists from Ecuador were being helicoptered in at a clearing about ten miles east of the compound. When he reported this to Sam, she told Brand, who confirmed to both that he was already aware of the fact. These movements were being monitored by the Peruvian military, and Brand had asked for a platoon of soldiers to be stationed adjacent to his laboratory. They did so without hesitation, as Brand's contributions to the Peruvian government were considered sacrosanct.

Shortly after breakfast, Brand asked Sam and Seth to join him in the conference room. Taking a sip of coffee, he said, "My sources tell me that there are no legitimate scientific expeditions going on near here that are sanctioned by any credible organization. So, they agree with me that this is likely the Sephtis group headed this way. Within the hour, a platoon of Peruvian soldiers will be arriving here. They are going to pitch tents and bivouac here until we put this threat behind us. In a few days, I expect we may retreat to our facility deep in the jungle to wait things out."

Seth smelled his coffee and seemed to revel in the experience. "Why don't you just ask the military to go to the spot where they are known to be arriving? Wouldn't that be easier?"

"We don't know how many are coming, and we want to be sure we get all of them," said Sam matter-of-factly.

"Why not just send a bevy of killer drones their way?" Seth asked, looking at Brand.

"We have to know for sure who we are dealing with, and it would be in our best interest to capture as many of them alive as possible."

"Well, I hope this doesn't take long. I still need to get back home and get on with what's left of my life, which isn't easy, knowing how desperately Sephtis wants me dead. Until they're decimated, I'm going to have to stay in hiding. If at any time enough members of the organization are left who have the means to pay the bounty, I'm in grave danger."

"I don't think you have too much to worry about, young man," said Brand. "I'm told that forces are at work that will soon cleanse the world of such a scourge, and not just Sephtis. Interface methodology has begun to make critical progress in finding groups that try to live off grid, outside of cyberspace. It's now possible to make reliable assumptions that these things are underway and making every effort not to call attention to themselves."

"I hope you're right," said Seth, putting his empty coffee cup on the table.

"Time will tell," said Sam. "Time will tell."

•◆•

Four days passed quickly. Seth's anxiety was growing, although he liked his accommodations, the food, the bed, even the occasional company. To pass some of the time, he had visited with a few of the laboratory scientists. While they would not discuss their work at the Brand facility, they proved to be fascinating conversationalists. Sitting in their break room one morning, Seth saw an Interface panel flash a notice that he was wanted in the main conference room.

"I've received word that the so-called botanists are headed this way," said Brand. "Our transportation is warming up, and we are about to head to the deep interior jungle, our home away from home. In America, you would call such a place your Camp David. Ours, however, is even more comfortable," Brand said with a smile, something Seth had rarely seen. "Go to your room and bring all of your gear. I don't know how long we will need to be there."

The helicopter was huge, the largest Seth had ever seen up close, with adequate room for him, Benjamin Brand, Sam, a chef, two scientists, and four security guards. Its speed was also impressive. No sooner had they reached their flying altitude than their forward thrust felt like a rocket launch.

The flight took a half-hour, and as Seth looked out, he could see nothing but miles and miles of dense jungle with a canopy so thick, it appeared one could walk on tree tops. Glancing through a window on the other side of the cabin, he could see what he assumed must be the Amazon River less than a mile away. What a place to be, though. Without this aircraft, he wondered if it would even be possible to get back to civilization.

On arrival, when Seth was shown to his living quarters, he was again impressed. Maybe it wasn't a Camp David, but it had to be close. The place seemed even more luxurious than the main headquarters, even though it was here in the middle of nowhere.

Sam said they would meet for lunch in an hour, so Seth took a shower and changed clothes. In the sweltering jungle humidity, the shower wouldn't have helped, if not for the air conditioning, and it would not do so now if he had to step outside. Walking down a corridor toward the aroma of a delicious lunch being prepared, he saw a picture window. From there, he could see another building about thirty yards away, a one-story building that was exceptionally tall and surrounded by concertina wire. This must be the place, he thought. This is where he or it lives.

Encounter

Since arriving at the deep jungle location, Seth had been asking Sam and Brand, whenever there was room for a question, when he might be able to meet the subject receiving so much attention. Each time, he was politely brushed off. So, this morning, having eaten earlier, he sat at the breakfast table drinking coffee when Sam and Brand took a seat. Almost as a routine request he said, "When do you two suppose I can interview the guest of much discussion?"

"How about eight o'clock?" Brand suggested.

Startled, Seth sat for a moment without speaking. "Okay, great," was all he could say.

"Come find me when it's close to time," Sam said.

When it was clear that his hosts were not interested in further conversation, Seth excused himself and went to his room. Bursting with exhilaration, he was surprised to notice that he also felt a bit nervous, almost as anxious as when he had interviewed the Sephtis leader. But here, there was no danger. At least he had no reason to believe there would be danger. He jogged in place, listened to music, and tried to calm himself with deep breathing.

At ten minutes before the hour, he called Sam, who met him in the foyer. She motioned for him to take a seat at a table in front of a large window. Once seated, she pointed outside to the tall building Seth had noticed earlier. "See that door over there, just past the gate?"

"Yes."

"I'm going to have the gate and door opened for you. Just go inside and introduce yourself."

"You aren't coming with me?"

"No."

"Why not?"

"It would just be better for you to go alone."

"I don't get it."

"You will. And don't be alarmed by the dog. One look from BenZ, and he will settle down."

"Dog?"

"Yes. Benzeerilla has a pet. His name is Max."

"What kind?"

"A Rottweiler."

"The hell he does."

Sam smiled and got up to leave. "Wait outside, and when you see the gate open, just go in and proceed." Then she left the room.

Seth sat in silence, stumped for words. He had asked so many times, and now suddenly he had the chance but was to go it alone. Okay, then. When he saw the gate open, he walked briskly through, opened the door, and entered.

Shortly afterwards, Sam returned to the table where they had been seated and opened a book to read. She wanted to be there when Seth returned. An hour passed, then two, three, four. At 12:30, Seth emerged from the neighboring building and walked slowly back. Ashen white, he started to speak, but his lips trembled and he said nothing.

"Sit down, Seth. Tell me what happened." She handed him a glass of iced tea, which he set back down on the table. His hands were too shaky to hold it steady.

"How did it go?" Sam asked softly.

"Jesus," he said. "Jesus."

•→•

Seth tossed and turned all night, never resting in one position longer than a few minutes before searching for another, something comfortable, someplace calm, peaceful, where he could forget what would best be forgotten. At daybreak, he rose only long enough to send an Interface message that he would not be coming to breakfast, that he wasn't feeling well and would be sleeping in. He went back to bed, but sleep he could not. Too much on his mind.

It was as if the depths of his psyche had been purged and laid bare. That before he was a serious, complicated man, now just seemed a juvenile notion. Seth who? And what the hell was he trying to prove? Why did the things he thought important before suddenly seem trite and unworthy, even as second thoughts? How had he managed to keep so many things buried in his subconscious? Could it be that this was a problem with everyone? Is believing we're the most intelligent species on the planet simply a ruse that we could now awaken from?

Shortly before 10:00, there was a knock on his door. "Seth, are you dressed?" Sam asked.

"Yes, come in."

"We missed you at breakfast. Are you feeling better?"

"I'm just tired, very tired from a sleepless night. Way too much on my mind after my session with *him*."

"Him? You mean BenZ?"

"Him, BenZ, however you want to characterize it. There is nothing to compare it to. I mean he's not God, but then, what *is* he? For the first few minutes of the meeting, I was simply frozen in place at the sight of him, and that voice seemed to echo and reverberate through my body, into and out of my bone marrow like microwaves in an oven. And those eyes. Jesus Christ, those eyes. Then, half an hour or so after I began answering his questions as best I could, the tears came so fast, I could barely see him. He seemed to know more about me that I have ever known about myself. When I said I'm a vegetarian and how fond I have always been of animals, his attitude toward me took a kindly turn. And when I told him about Rex, he suddenly looked at me with one of his eyes blue and the other one brown to match my own. I felt like a child on the first day of school."

Sam pulled up a chair. "Your reaction is not unusual, Seth. BenZ has not had many sessions with people other than the staff. He had long conversations with a young girl we hired to wait on him, but she never saw him under normal conditions."

"What do you mean 'normal conditions'?"

"The only time she saw him was when he rescued her from kidnappers after many months of talking to him every day through a one-way window. She didn't know what he looked like, and he frightened her. In any case, something about his ability to see through all human pretense and get to the core of a person's soul is truly unnerving."

"Unnerving, for sure. I'm still so addled that I can't quiet the spinning inside my head. It's as if he pulled my intimate thoughts about what I value in life out by the roots, and now I must put them back in order, but I don't know how because I don't know what order they were in before. I mean, that's the big deception with people, isn't it? We are all wound up and set in motion by a source of culturally internalized motivation that we don't have any sense of, and we fool ourselves constantly by coming up with nonsensical reasons for automatically doing things we don't understand. Isn't this true, Sam? Have I just lost it, or is this the dilemma of humankind?"

"No, I don't think you've lost it, Seth. What you have just described is very close to the reason for the existence of Benzeerilla. When Mr. Brand first told me about how Benzeerilla could thrust a mirror in humanity's face, I thought the whole thing sounded outlandish. But when you've been in BenZ's company for a while, it no longer seems farfetched. Have you ever heard of Jiddu Krishnamurti?"

"Sounds familiar. Refresh me."

"He was born in 1895 and groomed by an organization with the intention that he would become a world-class teacher, a guru's guru so to speak. Now, I know for a fact Mr. Brand was fascinated by Krishnamurti. He has never said so, but I expect that's where he got the idea that Benzeerilla would serve a similar function.

"Krishnamurti learned his lessons very well—too well, as it turned out. He concluded that truth cannot be given from one person to another, that we spend too much time in a cultural sleep, and the whole point of education is to wake up. He maintained that the more awake we are, the less we're likely to rely on belief, that negative thinking and skepticism are high-order thinking, and that, although belief seems to be a foundation for cooperation, it tends to make us prisoners to our emotions."

"What was the result?" Seth asked.

"What happened was that Krishnamurti turned against the very group who had supported him and provided him his continuing education. He decided he would not let himself be used by others. If he was against anything in the world, it was the idea that people need gurus, so he sure as hell didn't plan to become a caricature of one. I'm becoming concerned that we may be seeing something very similar with BenZ."

"How's that?"

"Everything was fine until we hired Pilar to wait on him, and he hasn't been the same since."

"You mean he has romantic feelings for a human? How unfortunate."

"I know Mr. Brand is worried about it, and he's angry with himself that it was something he hadn't even considered. It's the scientist side of him, I guess. Mr. Brand says..."

"Sam, you don't have to keep saying 'Mr. Brand.' I know you two have been living together for years."

Sam smiled. "It's a habit I don't want to break. Everyone here knows as well, but we like to keep it formal."

"Okay, I can respect that. I understand what you're saying about Brand's assumptions. What's hard for me to figure out is how Brand made such a leap of faith in the first place. How would he know how his creation would turn out? And what does BenZ mean to you?"

"BenZ means the world to me, but I can't answer your question about how Ben could predict such a thing. I can only point out that he is a very intelligent individual."

"Well, except for me, that seems to be prerequisite for being here. Odd man out, I am."

"Oh, I think you're a pretty smart guy. I suspect that when we look at BenZ, some of us see the absurdities in ourselves, thinking we are born free and able to exercise free will. When BenZ exposes the façade, we begin to realize that, however deeply involved we are in living our lives, our sense of control is nothing more than an egregious deception."

Sam waited for Seth to nod with understanding before she continued. "BenZ has made it clear to us that he believes real freedom is not having to choose, not being forced to make choices, so to speak. Do you know of anyone, ever, who just seemed to awaken one day from the trance of their life and walked away as if they were free to do so, beholden to no one? I suppose there are people who have a sense of freedom and feel completely unencumbered by any sense of responsibility, but I've never witnessed one."

"Good point, Sam. A couple of weeks ago, all I could think about—aside from avoiding assassination—was getting back on top in the news business. Now, after a few hours in a session with a one-of-a-kind being, I suddenly feel as if I've been taken apart and need putting back together. The only thing I know for sure is that I could not care less about getting back in the news business."

"You still want to do this story, don't you?"

"Yes, most assuredly. This is indeed worthwhile. If he can do for others what he has done for me, I can think of nothing I would rather do. But when this story is over, and if I can get the bounty off my head, I'm going to live in the woods of Tennessee among dinosaurs made of plants."

Blackout

Just after midnight, Seth was awakened by an alarm, a low-frequency buzzing noise with red lights flashing on random Interface screens. He dressed quickly and soon received an Interface message: "Seth, our military contacts have misread what the Sephtis group is up to. In the darkness, the attackers came close to the compound, were apparently met with boats on the river, and are headed this way. Our source says they could be here any time now. Mr. Brand thinks someone in the Peruvian government has deceived us on purpose. The military forces back at the laboratory compound anticipated an attack for more than two days. When it didn't occur, they should have known something was up."

"So, what do we do now?"

"Not much we can do but try to hold on until we get help. A military unit is on the way here. Their helicopters aren't as fast as our fleet, so it could be a while. Meet us in the conference room."

When Seth entered the small conference room, it was nearly full. Twenty people were present besides Sam and Brand, and eight of the group had on vests stamped *Security*, front and back. Brand said something barely intelligible, and Interface screens on the walls and ceiling came online instantly with a 360-degree view of the perimeter. Bright lights lit up the grounds for a hundred yards in every direction. No one spoke, as they all stared at the screens, searching for any sign of intruders.

Seth moved near Sam and whispered, "Is anyone with BenZ?"

Shaking her head, she said, "No, he is always alone. He insists that no one be in his presence without his approval."

On the river side of the compound, there appeared to be some activity, but it was too far away to be identified. Everyone focused on the movements. In an instant, they saw an armed man rushing toward the main gate. Brand spoke, and as soon as the man was close to the gate, a light flashed and a security drone nearly cut him in half. Seconds later, someone still hidden in darkness fired a rocket shell that hit at the base of the main gate and blew it open.

For two minutes, nothing happened. No movement, no sound. Then darkness. It was a complete electrical power failure. Battery backup lights came on shortly, both inside and out, but those on the outside lit only a few yards past the outer fences.

Brand spoke to one of the men wearing a security vest. "Do we have the capacity to put drones into action with just the battery power?"

"I honestly don't know, sir. We've never lost power this way before. We didn't think it possible with full redundancy built into the system. Whoever is doing this knows about the backup generators and how this place works." Moments later, the outside lights went dark.

Seth leaned toward Sam and said, "Can they get to BenZ? Or can he get out of there?"

"He can do either, if he wants to," Sam whispered. "Whatever he wants to do, nothing can stop him. I would have thought you'd know that by now."

·◆·

For half an hour, there was no movement outside. Inside, the lights on battery power were dimming from the sheer amount of wattage consumed to support so much equipment. Brand and two of the security men stood in a corner of the room talking quietly, but Seth couldn't tell what they were saying.

Without air conditioning, stifling heat was overtaking the room. Wielding a hand-held paper fan to cool herself, Sam took a seat beside Seth. "It shouldn't be much longer before the military gets here."

He started to say something, but suddenly the place became totally dark. The batteries had failed.

"That's just not possible unless someone has access into the system," Sam said.

Flashlights from the security personnel lit the darkness, and Brand told one of the men to bring additional flashlights for everyone else. The whole room went silent as noise could be heard outside the building. Brand whispered something to one of the security guards, who motioned for three others to follow him. Heavily armed, they slipped out the door. Brand whispered to Sam, "I'm going to warn BenZ," and then appeared to speak into a personal communication device.

Gunshots, one after another, broke the silence—automatic fire and the sound of hand grenades. Trying to see what was going on, Seth and Sam pressed close to a bulletproof window, but, aside from flashes of light from gun barrels, the scene was impossible to sort out. That they were under siege was obvious, but by whom and how many they couldn't tell. Brand opened a ceiling vent so they could hear better, but right after he did so, quiet followed again and lasted for twenty minutes that seemed like an hour. This time the silence ended with individual gun-shots and the sound of men screaming. Eventually, all was quiet again.

• ◆ •

At daybreak, Seth looked out the window to see what appeared like forty or fifty men approaching with weapons. Suddenly the lights came back on and Interface screens flashed with a message: "Mr. Brand, I'm colonel Achacollo. Is everyone okay?"

Brand went outside to shake hands with the colonel. Seth, Sam, and several of the scientists followed. A few yards past the building where BenZ was housed, they detected a large object. Upon close examination, they could see it was the bodies of ter-rorists stacked like cordwood—four men down, head to foot, and four across in the other direction. The pile was nine men high, which meant there were thirty-six bodies. The door to the over-sized building was open, but there was no sign of the occupant. Max the dog was found locked in the bathroom. Mouths gaping, the group stared at the bodies, unable to speak. They could only search one another's faces for an explanation.

"Jesus, Sam. What the hell? A stack of dead men? How the devil? What the devil? Who would do such a thing? Why?" Seth was dumbfounded.

Sam put her hand toward his face to silence him. "Do you really need to ask? You know who, and the why should be obvious as well. The how doesn't take much imagination."

"Why didn't they just kill him? And where in the hell is he?"

"Mr. Brand has been in touch with him. He is in the jungle nearby and will return when it gets dark. I'm sure they tried to kill him, but whenever he is outside, he is so frightful looking that he always dresses in full body armor, head to toe. It would be too dangerous for him not to because he scares people to death.

Anyone who is armed and doesn't know who BenZ is will likely shoot first and save their questions until the deed is done. He's been seen a few times, and in this part of the country, he's simply considered a mythic creature, a ghost or spirit or something, unconnected to our presence here."

"Does he go out often?"

"No, but there is a path out back that goes all the way to the river through heavy jungle vegetation. It's a couple of miles of winding trail, and he walks or runs it now and then. I'm not sure why he won't let anyone accompany him, but we've had glimpses of him running so fast, it's hard to believe his speed because of his stride. But then, so many things about him are hard to believe, you sort of get used to it if you're around him enough. Not many people use the path, and it tends to disappear from jungle encroachment. So, occasionally, BenZ takes a machete with him. When he returns, the path is clear."

"Why does he run?"

"Why does anyone run? For exercise, to relieve stress, and, for BenZ, to keep from going stir crazy, I suspect. Despite the carnage that he can leave behind when he's angry, he is tender-hearted. He also suffers frequent bouts of severe depression."

"Depression I can relate to," said Seth. "When I was an awkward and weird-looking kid, the other kids called me Seth-clops because of my different-colored eyes. I can't imagine what it must be like to be truly different from every other creature on the planet, though. No wonder he's depressed. I'm surprised he's not suicidal."

"We didn't understand well enough the nature of phyletic or evolutionary memory as distinguished from instinct in DNA sequencing. When BenZ is faced with danger, he has no control over his instincts. I think you might call it pure instinct. We have discovered that he is afraid of snakes, for example, and he doesn't like rain. There are several things we didn't anticipate."

"But why would he stack these men he obviously killed like so much cordwood? They look like they're ready to be rigged for longshoremen to sling them aboard a vessel. I don't get it, and I don't know how Mr. Brand is going to explain it to the Peruvian military."

"Well, you can bet there is a message in the act somewhere, and if you had been in BenZ's company all these years, you would be always ready to explain weird stuff. About everything BenZ does is for a reason. My guess is that the stack of dead men is simply a signal to those who would attack us that they can be dealt with just as easily as these men were: If you want to end like this, just keep it up."

"So, what do we do now, Sam?"

"Mr. Brand is planning to have BenZ appear soon in the U.S. before a congressional committee. In the meantime, we should probably leave this location altogether. Information came in a little while ago that more Sephtis insurgents are on their way here. You should confirm this with your sources, if you haven't already. We will need a place to stay out of sight for a while, someplace they aren't likely to suspect we would be."

"I have such a place," said Seth.

"Where?"

"In Tennessee. It's a 120-acre amusement park that I own. It's called the Kudzu Zoo, and it's almost ready to open. The place would be perfect for hiding. It has several buildings with very high ceilings and new living quarters. It also is fenced and remote, even though it's just a mile off the interstate highway. Let's go inside and I'll show you what it looks like via Interface."

Sam studied the aerial footage of the park and seemed encouraged. "This might work. I'll discuss it with Mr. Brand."

Kudzu

With a group that included Sam, Seth, and a team of security guards, Brand's organization took two aircraft to Tennessee. On arriving at a private airstrip in Nashville, they rented two large motor homes for transportation to the Kudzu Zoo property. Although the park was scheduled to open at the end of October, Seth had managed to persuade his nieces and nephew to vacate the premises until he told them to return. "Think of it as a well-earned vacation," he said.

Seth also contacted his shelter unit's administrator in Alaska to explain that he needed more than two weeks away. During the conversation, he was upset to learn that people in nearby shelter units had inquired as to his whereabouts. When he asked if he could simply be transferred to a shelter unit in Tennessee if necessary, he was told they would have to wait and see.

The drive from Nashville with the motor homes was a forty-five-minute trip, but it took an hour and a half because the vehicle BenZ was in had an extended roof, and the driver had to be careful approaching bridges and overpasses. Amid the fall leaves in full color, the zoo park was impressive to see. The area was heavily wooded except for the main trail, along which every bend and curve revealed a breathtaking surprise of towering kudzu dinosaurs, each with its vegetation trimmed to perfection and with solar-powered eyes that stayed lit after dark. The place was spooky in a fun sort of way.

After Seth took Sam and Brand on a quick tour of the park and facilities, they agreed that the location should be safe until time to head to Washington. The hook-ups available for camping vehicles would serve the motor homes perfectly. Both units were state-of-the-art, with Interface screens built into the walls. While the group waited, they would investigate everything possible about Sephtis connections in America, keeping the FBI, the CIA, and Homeland Security discreetly in the loop and remaining ever mindful that terrorists might find them at any moment. For the next two days, the whole group engaged in Interface research, all except the occupant of the second motor home. Who was to say what he was doing?

On the third morning, Sam got a message from Omar in Peru. He said that Pilar had been calling nearly every hour or so, wanting to speak to Mr. Brand. He asked what he should tell her. When Brand learned of this, he said to transfer the next call and put her through. Shortly afterwards, the call came.

"Mr. Brand," Pilar said softly, sounding more than a little timid because she usually talked to Sam and seldom ever to Brand.

"Yes, Pilar, Sam is here with me. What can we do for you?"

"I don't really know, sir. I mean, I feel so bad. I'm so embarrassed about the way I reacted when I saw BenZ. If only I had known. It was such a shock. He has become the most important person in my life. If you had told me what to expect, maybe I could have been prepared, but now I don't even know what to say, and no one will tell me if I can ever see him again. What can I do, sir?"

"I haven't decided yet, Pilar. I'm not sure. BenZ has been severely depressed ever since he rescued you from the kidnappers. I'm sorry we didn't tell you before about his identity. We have been obsessed about security, and I'm sure you can now imagine why. BenZ is going to make a public appearance soon, and right now I'm very worried about him because he is still brooding. So, I must tread carefully about even mentioning your name."

"Could you please tell him I'm sorry about the way I acted and that I want to see him again?"

"Of course, Pilar. When the time is right. Anything you want to add, Sam?"

"Yes. Pilar, ask Omar to help you get a passport right away in case we want you to come here. I will also contact him with instructions. It will only take a day with our connections in Peru."

"We will contact you again soon, Pilar," Brand said. "Bye now."

When Pilar vanished from the screen, Sam said, "So? What do you think we should do about her? Should we tell him that she wants to see him?"

"I wish to hell I knew," said Brand.

Madam President

Marvin Winthrop was still wondering how long he would survive as director of the CIA with Olivia Bentley as president. She seemed to delight in needling him. Marvin suspected she knew that his politics didn't match her views, not even close, but in his job, that wasn't supposed to matter. In her position, people who agreed with her seemed to be the only thing that did matter. He had been sitting outside the Oval Office for three quarters of an hour and growing angrier by the minute. No doubt the waiting time was an expression of her power, just for him. Finally, the door opened and he was ushered in.

"Good morning, Marvin," President Bentley said with a smile much more animated than usual, making him shudder. It was a staff observation commonly agreed upon that when Olivia Bentley smiled with enthusiasm, it meant she was pissed.

"Good morning, Madam President. Nice to see you again." His face reddened slightly because he sensed that she knew he was lying.

"Marvin, I'm told that Benjamin Brand has been cleared of treason charges, and I'm actually glad about that. We don't need a stock market scare. I also understand that you've agreed to let him bring his Frankenstein monster here to address a joint congressional committee. I'm glad about that, too," she said, watching his face. "Don't look so surprised, Marvin."

"Madam President, Mr. Brand is convinced he is doing the world a great service. I know the rumors have been festering for years that he has created a moral blasphemy of epic proportions, but I must say, he seems to me a very decent man with good intentions. He is, after all, supposed to be a genius, so maybe we will be pleasantly surprised."

"Oh, there is going to be a surprise, Marvin, a surprise indeed. We are going to let Mr. Brand show off his freak and then we are going to cage it, as per animal regulations. We'll keep it under lock and key until we can arrange to have it euthanized as a humane and moral public service. Do I make myself clear, Marvin?"

"Yes, ma'am, but . . ."

"No buts, Marvin. See to it. And one more thing. You have this committee circus set for October 28. I want it changed to Halloween for effect. We'll showcase the monster."

"Changing the arrangements is not going to be easy."

"Easy is not the point here, Marvin. This is a matter of human ethics. Once this creature embarrasses the Brand image, we will be doing the right thing for the right reasons."

"What about the terrorists, Madam President? The situation is urgent. We need to act."

"I don't want them picked up yet. Our field cameras will keep an eye on them. Important things first, Marvin. For decades, this country has been marching toward moral bankruptcy. Now we're going to do an about face and head in the other direction, starting with our American citizen Mr. Brand, who has spat in the face of God. You read me, Marvin?"

"Yes ma'am, I do." President Bentley's posture made it clear the visit was over, so Marvin nodded and walked out feeling slightly nauseous at the thought that he might not be able to stop a terrorist attack in time. His warnings were being ignored.

Zoo Park Visitors

Seth's kin were happy to hear that he and the Brand group would be leaving Tennessee two days before Halloween, allowing them to open the zoo park on that day as originally planned. So, they set about changing the copy on Interface social media to announce the grand opening, and they reinstated their ads to appear in vehicles approaching the interstate turnoff to the zoo.

Wanting to make sure that all was as it should be and that his nieces and nephew had seen to everything he had requested prior to opening, Seth decided to have a look around. Sam accepted his invitation to go along. They began at the entrance in an off-road Honda, puttering along at a mere two miles per hour. The sun was about to set, and leaves trickled to the ground in every direction. The light breeze and the shimmering kudzu made the towering creatures seem to come to life.

"This park was an incredibly good idea," said Sam.

"Thanks. You should have heard the hoots and hollers when I announced plans for this place. Kudzu can grow nearly a foot per day, which means expansion is quick and easy but maintenance is continuous."

"Well, it does sound weird until you see it. These creatures seem eerily real. The breeze gives them life, and these woods are beautiful, especially with the changing leaves. I think this will be a big success. Have you thought of coloring the leaves to give each creature its own look?"

"We're working on it," said Seth. "I bet your laboratory could splice the plant genes and have them do it on their own."

"No doubt it could probably be done," Sam agreed, "but I think this place is going to work in any event. Every kid who passes by is going to nag their parents into coming here."

They turned a corner and were confronted with three brontosaurs appearing to feed on the leaves of trees. Seth pointed to a group of raptors nearby. "I hope you're right. I just want to be able to move about freely here before long, without having to be paranoid that assassins are lurking in every shadow. So far at least, on this whole trip, my security defense protection has not gone to alert status. Funny, but that bothers me too. Can't get rid of the idea of my head being featured on a platter, with Interface video and background music, and someone becoming rich because of it."

Sam shuddered. "Gross thought."

"Yes, but true, every word."

They came to a straightaway with Jurassic creatures in every position imaginable on both sides of the road. Wanting to change the subject, Seth assumed his journalist role. "Why don't you tell me more about how you got together with Benjamin Brand?"

"Hmmm. Well, I met him at a conference in Geneva many years ago. I was on holiday, having just received my PhD. As you know, Ben is a bit aloof, but he was nice to me and he also happened to be the most intelligent person I had ever met, something that's still true with one exception. So, he took my number, and after I got back home, he called and offered me a job with a salary much higher than I ever expected to receive, even after years of work."

"Weren't you freaked out when he told you what he wanted to do?"

"Yes, as a matter of fact, I was. But Ben is a very persuasive person, and I could always tell that he had the best of intentions. First thing I knew, we were more than employer and employee. The years flew by and here we are."

"How long before you started to make progress with the work?"

"We had several years of disappointing results, but no one will ever be able to appreciate the extent of the research and decisive tinkering of DNA that we achieved. BenZ's brain is a third larger than ours, his hearing is far superior to ours, and he can see extremely well in the dark. His hands are designed for maximum strength and flexibility, and the strength in his arms and legs is quite frankly unbelievable, scary even."

Seth laughed. "Do you know how frightening this will sound to lots of people, maybe most of the people in this country or even in the world?"

"Yes, I'm aware of the fear that such power suggests. What we didn't count on was that we had no real control over personality. BenZ is kind, empathetic, compassionate, caring, and more thoughtful than anyone ever, but when he is attacked or when someone he cares about is in danger, well, you've seen what he can do. When he feels threatened or when he gets angry, he can't control his rage. He just goes instantly insane. We didn't foresee that, or we would have tried to code against it."

"Jesus, yes," said Seth, shaking his head. "A stack of dead men, dead wood. I still can't get that picture out of my mind."

They rounded a bend and came face to face with a Tyrannosaurus Rex, mouth open, orange eyes aglow and flashing in the evening sky. "Why the name Benzeerilla?" Seth asked. "And why is he so tall? In a way, it sounds almost like an insult. Maybe that's too strong a description, but do you know what I'm getting at?"

"I do, actually. It was all BenZ's idea from a very early age. He insisted. I'm not sure we fully understand or can possibly understand what it's like to be the only creature of your kind on the earth. As for his height, our attention to multiple possibilities for making his legs right for walking and running affected his height more than we had anticipated. You simply can't imagine how much discussion and heated argument went into the selection of DNA sequencing for BenZ. He is truly one of a kind."

"One of a kind, hard to find a parallel," said Seth. "Eight decades ago, John Glenn was the first man in space. I guess BenZ's been in space his whole life."

"Well, I suppose he may as well be from outer space. He's an alien, no doubt about that. Despite all our expertise in psychology, we still come up short trying to explain the actions of an entity for which there are no comparisons. We argue a lot among ourselves at the lab. But it may be the case that only BenZ can explain BenZ. I wish you could have met David Cruz. He could explain BenZ better than any of us, even Ben."

"I've heard of him but never met him. Likewise, I wish you could have known JD."

"Me too."

Still full of questions, Seth asked, "Whatever prompted you folks to give BenZ the ability to change his eye color at will?"

"That was Mr. Brand's idea. He always imagined how startling it would be to talk to someone who could do that. But when we created the DNA coding for multiple eye colors, we had no idea that BenZ would be able to change his on cue, simply with a thought."

"Brand was certainly right about it being startling. I almost jumped out of my chair when Benz said something to me in an angry tone and his eyes flashed red. Sometimes he would change his eye color when he changed the subject, other times when I think he suspected I was not being honest or not listening closely enough."

"That's perceptive of you, Seth. I'd say you're correct in those assumptions. Imagine how he is going to come across speaking to a congressional committee."

"I'm at a loss about what to expect."

"As we all are, except Ben. He thinks BenZ will make his point, but the rest of us are not so sure." Inhaling deeply, Sam took in the otherworldly scene before her. "Well, it won't be long before we find out. We'll be driving to D.C. in the morning. Ben likes that idea better than trying to conceal BenZ being transferred to and from an aircraft."

"I can understand that. You know, these motor homes are the most livable accommodations I've ever experienced. They have everything a person could want."

"Ben noticed how much you like them. He asked me to tell you that, if you see us through all the way with your assistance on this venture, he will purchase one of them and give it to you as a gift in appreciation for your efforts."

"Jesus Christ, Sam. I'm stunned. I'm not sure what to say. These things must cost at least a million each."

"Close, Seth, close."

They were near the turnaround point to follow the trail back through an army of different creatures and past two drive-by refreshment stands all set to open. Seth stopped and motioned Sam to follow as he opened the door to one of the stands. "This should be capable of serving lots of coffee and food on the fly, don't you think?"

"Yes, very impressive. You've obviously given this place lots of thought. Your menu even has T-Rex burgers. Amazing."

As soon as they stepped outside and Seth was about to seat himself in the Honda, his ball cap began buzzing. "Jesus, they found me."

• ◆ •

The buzzing noise continued for two minutes as Seth drove at higher speed. "Keep looking around, Sam, and see if you see anyone."

"Could it be a false alarm?"

"Possible, but I doubt this is one of those times. These guys are well financed. Funny that they haven't fired any shots, though. Maybe their software can detect my protection service and they don't want to waste a shot."

When Seth speeded faster, the buzzing stopped. "Maybe they're just playing with me, trying to make me worry as punishment. You must know how sadistic these people are. As soon as we get back to a screen, I'll put Amy to work on it. What scares me is what might happen to my nieces and nephew when they get back here tonight, assuming Sephtis has figured out how we're connected. If those guys know I'm here, hell, they must know everything. Jesus, Sam, I'm not sure what to do now."

"Let's run it by our security detail and see what they can come up with."

"Okay. Maybe we should head out early." The encroaching darkness mirrored the worry Seth felt. As the breeze picked up, the swaying trees and their shimmering leaves added further weight to the dilemma.

A security man let them in when they reached the door of the motor home where Brand was working. "My security alarm went off a little while ago," Seth reported.

"Yes, we know," said Brand as he came to meet them. "Our sensors have just now detected three people in the woods nearby. We are tracking them, and I have alerted BenZ's security detail."

Seth sat down in front of an Interface screen and went to work. Brand sent him a screen showing a grid map of the area that contained infrared signatures of three persons in the woods a few yards behind the motor home where BenZ was staying. Two guards were clearly visible sitting by the door. Suddenly the infrared images appeared to burst into a run toward BenZ's motor home. Gunfire shattered the silence.

After a few moments, Sam said, "We have a man down. The door is open, and BenZ is outside."

•◆•

A gunshot wound to the neck had nearly taken the life of Mike Delany, a security man who had worked for Brand for more than a decade and was now hospitalized in Nashville. A KD drone had bounced off his Kevlar vest, or he would have died on the spot. His partner, Wayne Waller, was bruised but unhurt by the two bullets that hit his vest when the three terrorists attacked near Benz's motor home.

Wayne was only six feet tall and weighed less than two hundred pounds, so the Brand group had to put their heads together to explain how Wayne had broken the necks of three men. The state trooper who had answered the call couldn't stop staring at Wayne, clearly puzzled about how anyone his size could be that tough. Seeming unable to stay focused on the report he was writing, he looked at Wayne repeatedly, as if wanting to ask another question, but each time, he just shook his head and returned to his paperwork.

Before dawn the next morning, two motor homes and two SUVs headed east on I40, bound for Washington, D.C. Never since Sam had known Benjamin Brand had he seemed more depressed or more solemn than now. On the flight to Tennessee and during the time in the park, something was obviously bothering him that he wasn't willing to talk about.

As they passed through Knoxville, Sam said, "That was a close call. I don't know what we would have done if BenZ had been discovered. Can you imagine what those three fanatics thought when the last thing they saw was a giant? If we're not very careful, this whole plan will blow up before the committee meeting."

"How do you think they knew about the existence of the park?" Brand asked.

"They must have really broken JD before they killed him, the degenerate bastards," Seth said, looking out a window. "They must have, and knowing JD, he would have held out to the very end. There may not be much about me that they don't know," he added in a whisper.

Breaking News

Surrounded by a crew of security guards from various agencies, the caravan of motor homes and SUVs sat parked for the night near the new forty-story Capitol Tower, where the hearing would soon take place. It was late, but Sam, Brand, Seth, and a few others were engaged in various Interface activities at the back of one of the enormous vehicles. Suddenly, Seth said, "Look at this," and he pulled up a public broadcast that everyone could see.

A woman appeared at a desk with a row of Middle Eastern flags behind her. She spoke directly to the camera. "We have just been told that a creature which is part man, part ape, and part chimpanzee is set to appear before a joint congressional committee in Washington, D.C. We will bring you more news as soon as we have it. Stay tuned."

"How did they get that?" Sam asked.

Seth looked worried, thinking he might be the obvious suspect. A long silence followed and grew more uncomfortable by the minute, as everyone in the vehicle tried to look at Brand without drawing his attention. Finally, Brand stood up and said, "I leaked it. Stop worrying."

"But why, Mr. Brand?" Seth asked. "I thought we were keeping this a secret."

"Why do you think I would spend millions speculating about what Benzeerilla would say if I did not expect a big audience? I never intended to have a closed session if I could arrange an open hearing. I want the world to watch, and you, Seth, have the edge over all the world's reporters. They will take instructions from you because you will have first Interface distribution access. You should also know, Seth, that we purposely leaked information about BenZ to your partner JD. We had no idea he was in jeopardy. We knew the CIA was snooping around, but we didn't know we had traitors in our employ. I am deeply sorry."

Seth forced a half-smile, a little embarrassed that he hadn't seen this coming. He was glad the others wouldn't think he'd blown the whistle, but the news about JD was gut-wrenching. "It makes sense, sir." He leaned back to reflect a moment and then said, "I need to get some air. Sam, would you like to come along?"

"Sure, let me get a jacket."

Washington in late October didn't smell like the glorious woods in Tennessee, but the crisp night air was invigorating. Outside the motor home, it was obvious that government security personnel had them under observation. "Feels good out here, don't you think?" Seth rolled his shoulders. "I need to be distracted right now. I'm not sure how to process the news about JD. Did you know about the leak, Sam?"

"Yes, I'm sorry to say. It was mostly me doing the leaking, but I didn't do it in person."

They walked only a few yards before Seth said, "I need to change the subject. This Halloween weather makes me wonder, doesn't broadcasting this meeting on Halloween cheapen the whole thing in a way? I mean, how many people are going to think it's just a "War of the Worlds" stunt like Orson Wells pulled a century ago?"

"Well, the Interface is not radio. I think Ben was sort of annoyed that the government insisted on October 31, but after he thought about it for a while, he seemed to start liking the idea." Sam paused. "Ben has seemed so withdrawn lately. Have you noticed?"

"Yes, as a matter of fact, I've been wondering about it ever since we left Peru. I'm guessing he's probably just worried that, after years of work and several fortunes spent, this whole thing might not go as planned."

"I certainly hope our efforts aren't wasted. I've asked him several times what's bothering him, and he just brushes me off."

"Well, Sam, tomorrow we'll find out for sure what the big fuss is about, what Benzeerilla is going to say after all the hype. I must admit that the buildup is a public relations masterpiece. I just can't imagine anyone anywhere could say anything that would be worth the time and money spent. The cost must be in the millions and millions."

"It's up there, all right. I can't say if it will be worth it, only that Ben has staked his reputation on the idea. He thinks that the perspective of a one-of-a-kind species, a species superior to humans in strength and intelligence, can say things that become a reference point, a turning point in perspective. We will know soon enough. It will likely kill Ben if it doesn't work out. I don't mean literally, I just mean in spirit."

"Well, no doubt the expectations for tomorrow will be great."

"The only real expectations tomorrow belong to Ben. No one else has any idea what to expect, nor will they know what to think until they've had some time to reflect on what they see and hear."

Seth started to speak when a buzzing sound from his cap broke the silence. "Jesus! They're here too."

Quickly returning to the motor home, Seth went straight to an Interface screen and began searching. "Looks like a false alarm this time, Sam. There is so much security hardware around here that I'm getting false readings. It's about damned time for some good news."

The President's Request

I t was a beautiful morning, All Hallows' Eve. The slight chill in the air seemed fitting to Benjamin Brand for what lay ahead. He was not in a festive mood. Throughout the entire trip north, he had felt so sad as to be close to tears. As he stepped out of the motor home on his way to Capitol Tower for the hearing, he was met immediately by Secret Service agents who had a car waiting close by with a door open.

"Sir," one of them said, approaching him with credentials in hand. "Sir, the president wishes to meet with you before the hearing." Brand nodded and took a seat in the vehicle.

Entering the White House, Brand felt uneasy. This must be the double cross he was expecting. He had heard nothing from Marvin Winthrop about the Sephtis locations he'd provided so the president could act. That was a couple of weeks ago, and he had received no response. Maybe the information was bad. Maybe it had just been a diversion. What could President Bentley want with him this close to the hearing, he wondered, a hearing where he was supposed to give the opening address?

The closer he got to the Oval Office, the more concerned he became. Growing angrier by the minute, he knew he needed to calm himself or this meeting would end badly. Bentley might even call off the hearing. Ushered by a doorman into the Oval Office, he saw Marvin Winthrop standing near the president's desk.

"Hello, Mr. Brand. The president will be with us shortly."

"What is the meaning of this, Marvin? I'm due to give an address in half an hour."

"I can't speak for the president, sir," said Winthrop, looking away.

"You people are about to make a big mistake, Marvin."

"You may be right, sir. That's not for me to say."

A door opened, and President Bentley entered, extending her hand. "It's nice to finally meet you, Mr. Brand."

"The timing is not very good, Madam President, as I am supposed to begin speaking in a few minutes. If you will give me a screen, can I do it from here?"

"Your creature can speak for itself, Mr. Brand. You asked that we make it possible and I agreed, but the terms and conditions are mine. This thing you have created will be allowed to speak, and then it will be taken into custody and kept under lock and key until we decide what is to be done with it."

"Madam President, I gave you the locations of known terrorists in this country, and in Pakistan, in exchange for the courtesy of allowing me to proceed with my plans. You people agreed to my terms."

"I gave the order to attack and destroy the location in Pakistan this morning, and suspects from the locations in Detroit and Chicago are in custody as we speak. We have had them under surveillance for some time. I never fully agreed to your terms, as you call them, Mr. Brand, and if you will recall, neither did Marvin. He just didn't say no. But now I have. We will watch your circus act from this room, and then you may leave, but your abomination will remain here with us."

On Board

Pilar had only two hours' notice to get ready after receiving a message from Samantha asking her to come to Washington, D.C. The message said BenZ was to give an address before a congressional committee and that he had been so depressed and at times so despondent that she was worried about him. Samantha said that Pilar's presence would likely be what was needed to cheer him up. She would be accompanied by a bodyguard and taken to the place of the hearing immediately upon landing in Washington.

Pilar wanted to go, feeling it was her duty. BenZ had radically changed her life for the better, after all. She was no longer as shy, and she was much better educated than before. Now she had a deep and abiding thirst for knowledge. But every time she recalled that night when he rescued her, she became distraught. She could handle the reality intellectually but wasn't sure she could keep her composure upon seeing him again.

She wished she could talk to BenZ on an Interface connection first, but her access had been severed. Even though the entity that had stood before her that night was so strange looking, she could see that he was hurt. That much was clear. When she thought of all those months of wonderful conversation and his patience and kindness in helping her to understand more and more complex ideas, the image of the hurt on his face flashed in her mind and the remorse she felt grew more painful. Nothing she could ever do or say would be able to take the heartbreak of that night away from her mentor.

Now Pilar was nervous, never having been in an airplane before and never having traveled anywhere beyond her small village. Sitting next to her was a bodyguard who was nice but seemed reluctant to carry on much of a conversation. The plane was revving its engines, about to take off on a long flight. Well, she had always dreamed about going to North America to live. At least now she would find out how much of what she had dreamed was true. As the aircraft roared down the runway, Pilar clutched her armrests, shut her eyes, and imagined that this was all just a dream. For comfort, she listened on a headset to a recorded lecture of BenZ talking about the probable existence of other planets with living creatures.

Benzeerilla Speaks

OCTOBER 31, 2043

40TH FLOOR, CAPITOL TOWER

WASHINGTON, D.C.

Only three people in the room looked comfortable: Seth, Sam, and one of the Brand security men. The individual in the witness chair was taller when seated than most other people are when standing. He was wearing a dark suit and a burgundy turtleneck. His facial features were mesmerizing—his head ape-like but still significantly human—and his eyes flickered with light, perhaps as a way of communicating.

Hoping his voice would not convey the fear he felt, Senator Maynard Jackson said, "Mr. Vice President, ladies and gentlemen, I'm calling this meeting to order. Benjamin Brand was expected to give an opening address, but I'm told that he will not be doing so. I am simply to give the floor to our special guest. So, you may proceed, sir."

Everyone in the room locked their eyes on the big chair and braced themselves for what was to come. Among the senators present were seven women and five men, and among the congressmen were eleven women and thirteen men. Three conservative firebrands were in the group: Senator Diane Simpson of Oklahoma, Senator Bill Longdale of Wyoming, and Representative Hallie Barber of Texas. All three stood out, visibly agitated and uncomfortable that such a hearing was taking place and that they were obligated to take part in it.

The colossal guest looked around the room for a moment, attempting to make eye contact with each person present. When most turned away without meeting his gaze directly, he began. "Hello, ladies and gentlemen. Since my human father is obviously being prevented from speaking, I will proceed. You all seem tongue-tied at the very sight of me and cannot look me in the eye." The deep resonance of the voice was rich in tone but also frightening because it was so strong and commanding.

"My father would tell you he spared no expense in my education. I can read more than a thousand words a minute, and I recall at will whatever I wish. I've read most of the books used in your colleges and universities. I have direct access to my subconscious. Aside from these facts, my father would have given you a lot of reasons why he thinks that a creature such as myself—a creature whose animal nature is deeper and more obvious to you than your own, and a creature whose cerebral capacity is far superior to yours—would have something to say that you should want to hear and reflect on.

"You see, my father believes that humanity is the only disease that has ever evolved the ability to be its own cure. He thinks that by looking and listening to me, you will realize that mankind needs some slight genetic modifications to stay alive on this planet. He knows that the interactions of culture and genetics drive behavior. Culture, he says, is simply projected biology, or instinct driven by genetics and memetics. Some genes are definitive instructive plans, and some are just recipes awaiting a reason to be cooked. He is aware that many great scientists have warned against domesticating human nature, and yet he believes that, until you step in to take control of the code that drives your kind, you are all prisoners of metastasis. I say there are lots of metaphors to describe your effects on the planet, but none are sufficient. From my perspective, you are a thinking plague.'"

An audible stir surged through the room. Maynard Jackson shuffled the papers in front of him. Vice President Abrams coughed discreetly.

"You have a tainted history with eugenics to be sure, but letting ancient superstitious beliefs lead you to conclude that there is something sacred about random mutation is absurd. It is possible to tweak DNA code for specific reasons that offer dramatic improvements in the lives of individuals and society at large. Failing to do so, my father maintains, will be a serious breach of morality. He believes it is irrational to assume that chance is somehow sacred."

A few members of the committee began to whisper among themselves. Some appeared to be trying to get up the nerve to interrupt with a question or comment. The speaker paused for a moment as a way of inviting questions, but when none came, he continued.

"My father thinks it is foolish to depend upon natural carcinogenic mutation to render itself benign without scientific intervention. He believes cancer is simply genetic confusion and that if natural selection is so clueless and indifferent, then unnatural selection is morally fitting. To his thinking, the edict to love one's neighbor is a hill too steep to climb in the world of random metamorphosis. For people to be less willing to kill their neighbors simply because they can't agree on what constitutes reality would be a big leap forward.

"Instead of expressing horror at the thought of tweaking DNA, your horror should be reserved for what happens if you don't make some practical adjustments. Fine-tuning some of your defective predilections, to remove them from the menu of acceptable behavior, is like fixing potholes in a road—the ride will be smoother and you will have a better chance to get where you are going."

Vice President Abrams stood up and said, "Yes, but that means playing God, does it not?"

"Only if you believe in the divinity of ignorance and random mutation."

Abrams looked around the room in search of support, but no one spoke.

"Engineering a genetic bias to any degree, in any direction, is dangerous," continued the speaker, "but what about the moral blindness of psychopaths who do in the open what your species does by simply living absurdly without regard to the environmental consequences of your behavior?"

BenZ scanned the audience, pausing to look at each member directly. Few were willing to make eye contact. "Do you people think your job as individual members of your species is simply to propagate genes and keep the virility of your collective toxicity in play? Or do you bear some responsibility for the existence of psychopaths, given that you have the wherewithal to weed them out of existence? My father thinks that humanity still maintains the ability to shape the future. I don't, however."

Congresswoman Barber had both hands in the air, waving furiously for attention.

"You have a question, Congresswoman?" Maynard Jackson said.

"Yes." She stood facing Jackson instead of the guest speaker. "Why on earth would anyone bring into being this creature who is lecturing us today as if we are children?"

Before Jackson could reply, the guest began again. "My human father created a freak for effect so that you can see the possibilities and realize that you need not go as far as he has. Man can change with incredibly positive results. You see, I know my father better than he knows himself. He created me for subconscious reasons that he is barely aware of, but which should soon become clear to you—clear because your species is facing oblivion. That this is not obvious to you only serves to make my point."

Congresswoman Barber stared at Maynard Jackson with a smirk on her face and shook her head.

Looking directly at her, the guest continued. "You—your species, homo sapiens, mankind, humanity—you bear a fractal relationship with the very disease that has been killing your kind from the beginning of your time on the earth. You represent culmination points in genetic code. Every one of your species, every individual, represents a cancer cell, a manic individualist entity, whose actions metastasize geographically and destroy one natural environment after another. For the essence of organic life, humanity is cancer having become conscious. When your kind split the atom, you simply metastasized and radiation became an extension of the disease that is you.

"The number of different kinds of cancer cells in existence correlates rather well with the variety of toxic ways that humans choose to pervert the earth's natural habitat and thus invade new territory with mutations. In time, these give way to new and even more lethal forms of metastasis. You haunt this planet with leukemic results, ladies and gentlemen. You live to kill. You eat sentient creatures. You are devourers of life. You are, as was said many years ago, the 'destroyer of worlds.' Ironically, the poorest of your kind are the least toxic."

All around the room, people exchanged glances, waiting for someone to interrupt the speaker, but no one raised a hand.

"You speak of progress, you champion intelligence, and yet the most intelligent among you represent the most virulent cells, the most ardent killers, the vilest of the vile. Turning the resources of this planet into nuclear waste, your own chemotherapy for the treatment of cancer is thus itself ultimately carcinogenic. Earth is sick with deforestation, depleted ozone, air pollution. Dead zones in the oceans due to acidification are growing like weeds, and species disappearance has reached a rate higher than the world has ever seen. Human beings represent an extinction-level event.

"You are a serial-killer species, and yet this sphere of organic matter hurtling through space is self-regulating. In time, this planet will rid itself of your kind. You know, don't you, that the universe has remedies for your type of malignancy in the form of asteroids, comets, super volcanoes, gamma-ray bursts, and super viruses? Do you understand that I am an example of your metastasis? You see me as the freak I am, and I see you as you are. Do I make myself clear?"

The room was pin-drop quiet. The speaker's voice was so deep and resonant that the listeners' bones seemed to reverberate in convulsive shudders. The fear in the room was palpable. Benzeerilla appeared capable of killing anyone present with a simple backhanded slap.

"Human progress is an illusion. You see technology as advancement, but what you don't see clearly is the malevolence your so-called science represents. Your luxuries have become necessities, making you exceptionally dangerous and yet vulnerable. Even if your technology does not destroy the earth, the planet will nevertheless shed its surface of your kind. And this will likely happen by your own hand, because you have now achieved the technological ability as individuals to join the ranks of killer asteroids and gamma-ray bursts. One person can kill millions. Cancer cells are ultimate expressions of greed, and as such, they set out to kill their host in the same manner that you are killing the habitability of this planet."

There was a pause, and the vice president tapped his table gently with a gavel. "Thank you for your opening remarks, sir. Maynard, why don't we take a fifteen-minute break?"

"Indeed, sir. Good idea. We will resume in fifteen."

Positive Mutation

For nearly five minutes after the hearing called for a break, Benjamin Brand, Marvin Winthrop, and President Bentley sat motionless, still looking at the screen and seeming to avoid looking at one another. Finally, Brand said, "So, Madam President, I didn't hear you say anything while we were watching Benzeerilla speak. Has he said anything immoral, blasphemous, or somehow indicative that he is not much more than an animal that needs to be caged?"

"And what would you call him, Mr. Brand? What category does he fit? Do you consider this God's work? You heard how he views the concept of God. You don't call that blasphemous? And he doesn't seem all that enthusiastic about his very existence. It's not even clear to me how much he agrees with you. What if he doesn't live up to your expectations?"

"He has already exceeded my expectations, Madam President."

"Then you, as the creator of his life, does this make you God? Do you now see yourself as creating a whole new species in the image of what you think man should be? Do you intend that the future will be populated by superior beings brought to us by Brand International?"

Marvin cleared his throat and said, "She has a point, Mr. Brand. Several, if you are counting. The main point is what comes next, now that you have opened the gates to the creation of cross-species development? Do we have sheep-men, cat-people, humans with fins so they can win swimming contests? Don't you see what this opens us up for? Isn't there anything sacrosanct about humanity? Surely you are familiar with the notion a century ago of racial hygiene."

"Well put, Marvin," President Bentley said.

Brand spoke calmly. "Look, both of you are forgetting something here, something that should be obvious, something that should make this whole thing clear. This is not the racial hygiene of the Nazis. BenZ is in every way a superior being to man, in the same way that humans are far superior to worms, even though they have roughly the same number of genes. BenZ can show us the possibilities of real intelligent design through human ingenuity. The term *mutation* has a negative connotation, but positive mutations are real. BenZ can hold a mirror up to our kind in ways that have never been possible because he still eats, sleeps, dreams, smells, and sees through a veneer of animal nature that we can no longer experience. The architecture of his brain is an exponential leap in the direction of human evolution, many thousands of years ahead of the timetables that nature has required for our development. Can't you look at BenZ and appreciate him for what he is, that his being alive can be of great value to humanity?"

"For someone with a reputation for being a genius, you are incredibly naïve, Mr. Brand," the president said. "Nothing you have said makes up for your blasphemous breach of trust in having opened the door to sacrilegious acts in the name of science."

Anxiously pointing to the screen, Marvin said, "The hearing is back in session."

Pride and Empathy

Maynard Jackson looked at Congresswoman Barber, then around the room and asked, "Does anyone have any comments before we continue?" Silence followed. Clearing his throat, he nodded at the speaker. "You may continue, sir."

"You may call me BenZ, Mr. Jackson. My friends do." The smile on his massive face brought audible expressions of relief among the audience.

Interface social media forums worldwide were experiencing stratospheric activity. Commentators were describing it as "trick-or-treat news" while calling attention to the fact that this might be the most watched media broadcast in world history. At the far side of the hearing room, Seth was streaming commentary along the bottom of the video feeds, making it clear where the broadcast was originating and by whom. Every few minutes, the words *In Memory of Justin Davis* appeared on the line in small print.

"Please continue then, BenZ," Maynard said, smiling and feeling for the first time a sense of relief in what seemed like such a threatening presence.

BenZ softened his voice in a slightly higher octave, and his eyes flashed to green from orange. A murmur erupted in the

assembly of stunned onlookers. "Ladies and gentlemen, you celebrate the brain of your species as the world's most complex and
most sophisticated known entity, but that is no longer the case.
My brain is superior to yours in every way. It's larger, with two
frontal and two lateral sections that you do not have. I can dream
at will in algebraic formulae, calculus, trigonometry, and anal-
ysis. I can hear frequencies that you can't, like termites at work
in wood. I can see things invisible to you. My sense of smell is
greater than that of a bloodhound, and I can turn it on and off at
will. I can read body language in humans and animals in ways
you simply cannot conceive. I can tell which plants are edible by
sight and smell. I can foretell the weather hours in advance. At
night, I can see in the infra-red spectrum if I choose. You don't
have direct access to your subconscious. I do have access to mine
and more."

He stopped speaking for a moment and turned to face each
person in the room. Keeping his eyes on them until they looked
directly at him, he then immediately matched their eye color
with his own, causing loud gasps to ripple through the room like
distant thunder.

"You look at me and see an animal. You see correctly. My
apparent animal grounding is what scares you, and it's what gives
me a vital perspective that you do not have. You are animals who
prefer not to think of yourselves as animals. You think you are
far superior, and yet it is because you feel no genuine animal
empathy that your species is destroying the habitat for all the
species of life on this planet."

Diane Simpson jumped up from her chair and said, "That's
just not true. We already have too many people who are animal
rights fanatics in this country."

"No doubt, some of your species are empathetic, but not
enough of you feel the kind of true kinship with the other

creatures in this world that would make a real difference. For too many of your kind, the capacity for empathy for other species is in short supply. Your empathy as individuals is insufficient to make amends for the destruction you bring to bear from being estranged from your environment. Collectively, you should have figured this out by now.

"You continue to eat sentient creatures when you have plenty of alternative sources of food—nutritional, organic food that is much better for your health than animal flesh. You perceive yourselves to be the masters of this world, but instead you are the parasite eating away the thin membrane that makes life possible and sustains it. You do not understand that all animal life represents cognition—cognition as matters of degree in myriad expressions of perspective, while perspective can be as simple as a creature deciding what to do next. Such creatures feel hunger, fear, affection, warmth and cold, caution, uncertainty, and confusion, and yet they do not shoulder the responsibility of the future for all species. You, on the other hand, do.

"Two and a half centuries ago, you passed the tipping point of collective activities that will ultimately render your kind extinct, and you barely have that much time left. Even so, you are still blind to the threat you pose to yourselves and the other sentient life forms on this planet. My father wants to help you change direction, but I don't share his optimism that you can make a course correction. There is nothing any of your kind can do now to save yourselves. The best you can do is delay the inevitable."

Twisting in his chair, Vice President Abrams cleared his throat and said, "A most impressive opening, sir. But do you not owe your very existence to our animal nature, so to speak?"

"Mr. Abrams, sir, secretly you mock me, do you not? Let me reiterate. Your species, at this period, represents stage four metastasis. If you examine the health of this planet, this fact is undeniable. But what is not so clear is the great irony your existence symbolizes. Each one of you represents the very incarnation of malignancy, as I have said, and yet, in the eyes of the other creatures in this world, each of you is a god. To borrow from your mythology of Ancient Greece, you possess the powers of Zeus and Apollo over the lives and fates of conscious, sentient creatures—creatures that can experience joy and feel pain and pleasure. These are empathetic creatures who know fear, creatures capable of affection, who strive desperately to stay alive. They experience distress from the butchering of their own offspring, whom they recognize as kin, in their presence, as so often happens in the assembly lines of industrial slaughter factories. You are responsible for bringing into being the most miserable creatures who have ever drawn a breath.

"Your human savagery is far beyond the pale of nature that you so often characterize as being 'red in tooth and claw.' Your barbarity exceeds the agony and the irony of one animal engaged in the act of eating another that's still alive. So, spare me your girded animosity, Mr. Abrams."

"I mean you no disrespect, sir, or BenZ."

"Well, then, could it be that you cannot relate to life beyond your own kind because your cerebral connection with what you characterize as lower forms of animals has been severed? You watch animals behave in the wild as they act in unison without speaking, and so you assume there is no language. You do not see radio and television signals either, but you do not deny their existence. Animals plainly learn cause-and-effect association from experience, but you don't see it. Shoot at an animal that does not fear you, and the next time it sees you, it will run.

"You think of yourselves, all of you, as so far superior to the other creatures on this earth that you need pay their well-being no heed, none. A pleasurable taste on the tip of your tongue is of far, far more importance to you than the very lives of the animals that you feast on. So, tell me Mr. Abrams, Mr. Jackson, and Congresswoman Barber, why is the gulf between you and the creatures you depend on for your very existence so wide that you cannot fathom your cruelty—cruelty so horrific that words fail to capture even a semblance of the pain experienced? Why are all of you not vegetarians?"

Vice President Abrams started to speak, but a giant hand raised in the air meant hush. "When your species moved from hunter-gatherer tribes to agriculture, you moved from stage one cancer to stage two. Industrial society began stage three, and the information society—the Interface Society as you call it now—is stage four. You see, when you reach stage four, you have metastasized to a point where each cell has the strength to kill en masse, on its own, with the power of computer code. So, look around. As the influence of the individual increases exponentially, your risk goes up.

"Think about this fact: The point at which you become a success in the eyes of your society is the very point at which many of you begin to consume and waste with abandon for the simple reason that proving you can do so increases your perception of your social status. The great irony is that each paradigm shift I've mentioned that caused you to become more toxic to this planet is something you confuse with progress. With the discovery of DNA, your species should have realized that all life is algorithmic, and the knowledge that your code is more sophisticated than the codes of other creatures shouldn't blind you to their suffering, especially when your casual pleasure is the cause of their excruciating pain.

"Can you not conceive of just how morally blasphemous this kind of behavior is in the scheme of global karma? And think of the irony that your ancient ancestors had to be exceptionally knowledgeable to survive long enough to pass their genes on, whereas now, ignorant people, whom you call idiots, thrive and reproduce because the Interface acts as their brain. They are cyber-parasites begetting the mass reproduction of imbeciles. Your species is not growing more intelligent in time. The reverse represents your present reality."

Senator Longdale leapt to his feet. "Who, in the name of God, are you to be calling us idiots?"

"Had a god created life, senator, I more likely would be the rule and you the exception."

Another audible gasp swept through the room like an ocean tide. Muttering under his breath, Longdale exchanged angry glances with his colleagues and sat down.

"Think about the fact that human pride, especially false pride expressed as arrogance, amounts to a spike in malignancy. The very idea of humans seeking status and claiming superiority represents a viral scourge. You see, senator, I speak for myself. I do not represent a species. I'm a dead end, as all of you are soon to be."

Members of the committee were beginning to move about as if they had been seated too long, but most were unaware that their physical discomfort was not what was bothering them. Maynard Jackson took advantage of a brief lapse in the speaker's address to raise his hand and say, "Fifteen-minute break, folks."

•◆•

President Bentley rose from her desk and began to pace around the room as though she needed to busy herself. Pundits often commented that the president walked her worries away. She poured herself a glass of water and turned to face Marvin and Brand, who had stood up out of protocol. Sipping her water, she leaned back against the wall and said, "You still think that thing you have created is making your case, Mr. Brand?"

"Yes, Madam President, I do. I don't understand how anyone listening to his argument can dismiss it out of hand. Of course, no one wants to admit that humanity is at the end of its rope, but if we think he is wrong about this, the thing to do is to prove he is wrong by safeguarding the future."

"And let me guess, that's where you come in, Mr. Brand. No doubt you already have the remedy in a test tube, am I right?"

Marvin frowned and shook his head.

With his eyes on Marvin, Brand said, "What if it were possible, Madam President, to tweak the DNA of living individuals and render them more cooperative and more thoughtful and innovative at the same time? Would this not help curtail the inherent tribalism that keeps us at one another's throats all over the world and is routinely played out as genocide? Could we not mitigate our propensity to go to war over minor disagreements?"

When it was clear the president was not going to comment, Brand continued. "So, Marvin, what good is the CIA if your agency can't figure out how to deal with tribalism 101, and I have to do your thinking for you?"

Marvin stared at the carpet as if he had dropped something on the floor. He swallowed hard, took a deep breath, and said, "Surely, Mr. Brand, you don't intend that we vaccinate our way to utopia, do you, sir?"

Movement on the Interface screen showed that the assembly was about to resume, so Brand said, "Let's hear what else BenZ has to say before I answer your question."

Extinction

A few people were still walking to their seats as the hearing was called to order. Maynard Jackson and the vice president stopped whispering to one another, and Jackson said, "Please proceed, Mr. BenZ."

"Too many of your kind cannot face life without drugs. Is this fact not a clue that you have reached a cul-de-sac of fate, as the Ancient Greeks might have put it? Do you not understand that depression is a signal that action is required, even as you solve complex problems in this country with medication? Can you not reason your way forward to the conclusion that you are witnessing an example of poor planning, if a deity planned evolution on this planet and 99 percent of the species so far have become extinct? Can you not conclude that, instead of a thoughtful design, this cosmic domain is but an accident in a hostile and ungodly universe where chaos rules? Do you not see that your sense of morality is corrupted by the advantage you must maintain simply to compete to exist? Can you not think these thoughts, Mr. Abrams and Mr. Jackson and the rest of you present? Are you unaware that your kind has eaten one another as needed on occasion to get this far in time and will likely do so again if necessary? Can you not look at me and wonder if it may be possible now to create DNA that is morally inclined by design?

"Ask yourselves what the result would be if your kind could learn to want what you really need. Of course, the sad truth for your species is that, up to now, it's only because of the confusion over your wants and needs that your survival has been possible. You should know this without need of explanation because of your stealth religions of capitalism, socialism, and communism.

"What if you could avoid major diseases? If your progeny could be more intelligent than what random mutation can offer, would it not be prudent to ensure it? If a few changes in code could assure that your children would be born musical prodigies with perfect pitch, would you not choose it?

"Can you not appreciate that, for more than 99 percent of the time your species has been alive on this planet, your ancestors were hyperaware that they were morsels on the food menus of beasts? Being consumed meant nonexistence, and yet you are incapable of applying the lesson of awareness to the animals you have domesticated to consume. Do you not realize that each of you represents an unbroken chain of existence that goes all the way back to the beginning of life in the pond shallows on this planet?

"Since you have evolved to have intelligence enough to appreciate the unwitting damage your mindless activity is having on the continuation of life, does it not concern you that you are sleep-walking at your peril and that you are taking an untold number of species with you toward extinction? Are you so detached from the other sentient creatures of the world from which you have evolved that you feel no responsibility toward the sanctity of life itself?"

Diane Simpson raised her hand, and before Jackson could recognize her, BenZ said, "Yes, senator?"

"What makes you think that all of us don't care about the other life forms on this planet? Many of us care a great deal."

"I will grant that not all human empathy is lost, senator, but such sentiment only delays the inevitable. Has it never occurred to any of you that the DNA that links you to the simple amoeba of pond scum is by far more sacred than the idea of an invisible soul? Your wistful illusions are nothing but a lament that the chain of life you represent will soon be broken by your demise and that the part you played was not a big one. Do you not realize that you use religion to avoid life and that, in doing so, you bring death to most of the examples of life? No sentient creature can truly know its own nature, not even me, but to welcome illusion as a relief from reality is to worship irresponsibility. Can you people not comprehend this?

"Your religions are masks to quell your fears of death. Can you imagine a being in the future who is unafraid of death, a creature of great intelligence, for whom acceptance of the inevitability of nonexistence is, if not comforting, at least something not to be so feared that it leads to horrific deeds for distraction? Your religions amount to little more than desperate attempts to deny reality. They are socially aggressive movements to escape reality by offering rewards that violate the laws of physics. The whole idea of a soul is nothing save an illusionary cure for mourning. Can you not truly appreciate your predicament? The assumption of immortality is the epitome of arrogance because it results in wars about the nature of reality. The carnage is testimony to the toxicity of your existence."

BenZ leaned forward abruptly and spoke in a deep, commanding voice. "I heard that, Senator Simpson."

Simpson looked at the speaker and then around the room as if she had been caught cheating on a test.

"Senator Simpson just whispered to a colleague that I belong in a zoo. A rather arrogant and anxious statement, I suppose. Every age of human existence, senator, bears the same level of anxiety about the insecurity of the future because of the awareness it bestows that the future is nonexistence. Do you not understand the part that mortality salience plays in your culture, that it creates a desperate need for distraction?

"Can you not appreciate the price your species pays for being unwilling to face your own mortality without the need to blame others for it? Are you unaware that thoughts of your own mortality are never far from rising to full consciousness, like a volcano with a pent-up need to vent ash? A genuine respect for the inevitability of death could benefit your species as no other idea can or could. Are you not aware that it's unlikely you will ever achieve such a realization without some genetic modification?"

Two congressmen got up and left the room, one shaking his head and covering his ears. The speaker was not deterred.

"Do you most fear a loss of the future or the loss of the past? Think. Do you not understand that the ownership of property carries with it a longing for permanence, that your species is bedeviled by the anxiety of this existential desire, and that the more you own, the easier you are to manipulate? Do you not believe your ancient philosophers who have so carefully cautioned you that the best way to live is to prepare for death? Do you not understand that being shadowed and stalked by death is what gives meaning to the brevity of life and to the value of the lives of other creatures?

"Do you not understand that obsessive religiosity represents a fanatical fear of nonexistence and that such anxiety produces a never-ending supply of nonsensical beliefs? Do you not understand that those who seek power over you use your fear of death to do so? Can you not perceive of oblivion as Nirvana? Do you understand the lure of symbolic immortality and the concept of making a social contribution as a means of prepaying the tax on your existence, Mr. Abrams? Can you imagine anything more horrifying than nearing the end of your life and suddenly realizing that you have never lived or that your past willingness to submit to and obey the political authoritarians in power was your means of avoidance? Have you ever thought of listening to the screams of your subconscious, sir?"

Maynard Jackson threw both hands in the air and said, "Break time. We will resume again in fifteen."

His Presence

A gentleman met Pilar and her bodyguard at the airport. The driver of the waiting car seemed nervous. They needed to hurry. Pilar was not exhausted physically from the trip, but seeing so much that was totally foreign to her was sapping her strength. They were repeatedly stuck in traffic, in lines of countless cars, most with no drivers. Finally, on reaching the Capitol Tower, she saw Samantha Tyson on the steps, motioning to her to move quickly.

"Oh, Pilar, I'm so glad you're here. The hearing has been adjourned for a break and is about to start again. Someone is waiting at the door to let us in. We need to hurry."

Once inside and seated, Pilar tried to remain calm and in complete control of her emotions as she looked directly at the occupant in the speaker's chair. Seeing him so tall in a sitting position, it was hard not to think back to the first sight of him the night he tore the door off the hut she was in. Wearing a suit instead of body armor, he did look less menacing, but he was still clearly not from this world—enormous, with the frightening stature of a mythic god.

In his suit and turtleneck shirt, and with his coarse hair coiffed, BenZ could have been a postmodern work of art. His shoulders, arms, and chest looked like a granite bust, something in the imagination of an artist gone mad. Such power in one body made others feel powerless and small. Noting the armed men at the entrance, Pilar realized that the people in the room were scared. Their fears could easily be justified by what this giant presence could do if he were riled.

It was his face, though, that she was stunned to see clearly, his expression revealing him to appear more human than ape or chimpanzee. His head was huge, his forehead broad, his brow slightly arched, and his eyes mesmerizing. When he caught your gaze, it seemed as if he could lock you in at will, inspiring fear or empathy.

No longer revolted by his appearance, Pilar was not afraid. She could get used to the way he looked. There could be no romantic attraction as she had once imagined, but they could be close friends. She could be in the room with him and not stay hidden. Glad now that she had come, she thought this whole thing could have been so much easier had they just told her up front what they were doing. But then, when she thought back to the person she was before her time with BenZ, she understood that it might not have worked if she had seen him too soon.

When Pilar whispered something to Sam, BenZ looked immediately in her direction. The expression on his unearthly face was hard to interpret. Was it pain, pleasure, or some measure of both? His reaction made Sam wonder if asking Pilar to come was such a wise thing to do after all. Maybe not. It was now crystal clear why so many armed guards stood just outside the room like a SWAT team convention. They weren't here strictly to keep people safe, they here to get BenZ. Fear for the latter rose quickly in her mind. Where in the devil was Brand? Why had he not given an opening statement, and why was he still not here?

Across the room, Seth was staring at Pilar. From the moment he first saw her he'd had trouble keeping his eyes away. Thank goodness she hadn't noticed, because he wasn't sure he could stop.

Goodbye Pilar

When he finished talking to one of the security men near the entrance, Maynard Jackson returned quickly to his seat, winked at the vice president, and said, "Mr. BenZ, please resume."

"My father thinks you should be interested in my opinion, but he is mistaken. Your species consists of millions of individuals who believe that human beings, and only human beings, will live forever after their brains have rotted and decayed, all because of shared beliefs and illusions of specialness that portend doom for all other forms of life. Need I continue telling you the extent to which I hold such simplistic idiocy in contempt?

"Everywhere you look, there are examples of what life requires to thrive. The plant and animal worlds exist because their continuing actions sustain them. Plants and animals live and die in a nourishing process that pays the tax of their existence. But you—you the creature calling himself man, the superior intellect—you don't pattern your existence after the organic process that makes life possible. No, instead, you emulate one of the most destructive processes in biology. You employ greed with the same methodology that produces the devastation in cancer.

Your superior intelligence is made irrelevant by your unadulter-
ated greed. I repeat ad nauseam: Human beings are the greatest
threat to life on this planet."

Tilting his head toward an earpiece, Maynard Jackson was
visibly anxious. Finally, he stood and said, "Mr. BenZ, I'm being
told we have literally hundreds of thousands of listeners to this
broadcast who want to hear what advice you might have for ordinary folks."

BenZ thought for a moment and looked skyward. His eyes
turned the color of brackish lake water after a winter storm.
"Ordinary citizens, you say? Think of what it means to be extraordinary. What do you think makes others extraordinary? Learn,
learn, learn, until those who share your company begin to think
you are insanely articulate, out of touch, on a planet of your own
creation. Then, and only then, will you begin to fully appreciate
what it has meant to be alive, to have grasped at fleeting straws of
meaning in a meaningless universe, to feel a slight semblance of
illumination in the dark of a cold and utterly indifferent cosmos.
This is as good as it gets for sentient creatures with your limited
gray matter, and yet few of your kind venture to such heights in
the short time that you live. Your sensory perceptions are frail,
but still you make little use of what you have. Most of you spend
your lives reacting to cues that you aren't even aware of.

"Your lives are like sparks in a dark cosmic void. You are here
in the blink of an eye and gone in another. If, during this time,
you awaken to comprehend the wonder and chance of your existence, even for a moment, it makes you one in a million. Each of
you is a link in the chain of existence, an umbilical cord bound
all the way back to primordial waters, and yet you do not fully
appreciate the connection. If you did, you would not turn a blind
eye to the mindless degradation of the earth and all the fellow
creatures who are your relatives. You should feel lucky, blessed

even, because you have the power of gods, which your distant kin did not.

"To truly experience the rewards of being alive, you must feel that you belong, but you must also be able to see through the illusions you have learned to depend on. All life lives at the expense of life, and thus living without exploitation is not possible. But living without an awareness of such a tax on one's existence leads to irresponsible actions. Until you learn to see what is before you and not what is said to be before you, you cannot learn to think clearly, and time becomes your unacknowledged but persistent enemy.

"Most of you fail to be aware of the price your species pays because time is a relentless taskmaster to mortal beings. But it's not so much that you are unaware, or that you are simply in a hurry to do things. It's that you can't comprehend how the psychological effect of the taskmaster rules your lives in such a way that you become puppets to your worst instincts.

"Like playground children, you redirect your fear of time running out onto the members of your own species that you deem to be different enough to qualify as being the *other*. If the universe is rife with living beings, as I suspect must be the case, then surely you rank in the lower echelons of intelligence because you are crippled by infantile emotions that guide your behavior.

"Many of you erase any possibility for a meaningful existence because you mistake busyness for purpose and you devalue those whom you believe are idle. You fear death because you imagine that it robs you of the future. But at a subconscious level, what you fear most is losing the past. You look at me and see an abomination. I look at you and recognize that you don't see yourselves in a similar light simply because you have chosen to live in the shelter of illusion.

"You are so incredibly naïve that when you look out at the world, you believe you see it as it is, which is patently absurd. What you perceive as being reality is the result of your limited cerebral apparatus, which is but a rudimentary sensory attempt for making sense of the world. A lack of curiosity manifests itself as the essence of malevolence because your instincts no longer match your environment. By clinging to superstitious beliefs, you cripple your ability to cooperate beyond a small group of like-minded believers.

"As humans, when you die, you will do so knowing that your kind will continue, at least for a time. Do you have any idea what it would be like to be born the only kind of your species? No, of course you don't. You think you understand loneliness? You have no idea. To be totally alone is not to be, in the sense of existence that you are accustomed to.

"Most of you do not understand the subconscious but symbolic need you have to share in being connected to your own kind's continued existence. This connection runs even deeper than your fairytale illusions of life after death. It is your slavish dependence on these feelings that causes you to fear nonexistence. If you fully understood the connection, you would not be so fearful of dying. You would realize that the moment when your kind is no more, the organic exploitation inherent in nature will continue. There will be a gasp of remorse, but it will be drowned out by a thunderous end to orchestrated suffering of such magnitude that it will echo for eternity.

"By the time your species collected enough data to tell you how to sustain your civilization, it was already too late because the deadline was past. Your time on this planet, which you refer to as the Anthropocene, is a history of devastation and missed opportunity. But now, your future casts a small shadow. You are experiencing the December of your species' existence, as am I.

And thus, there is not that much more I can tell you, ladies and gentlemen, except that you may delay the inevitable demise to come but you cannot stop it. You can, though, enjoy what time you have left if you awaken to the pain your existence requires of the other creatures of the world and if you try to lessen the needless pain they suffer. Considering that so much suffering derives from your existence, you misunderstand the heavenly peace that nonexistence will offer. If you understood the true meaning of the absence of suffering, you would not fear death. With that, I now bid you farewell."

When it was obvious that no one else would be speaking, BenZ rose from his chair. The sight of him standing at his full height was still a shock, even to those who had seen it before. He had expected Brand to be present. But because he had not received any private Interface messages from Brand for the duration of the hearing, BenZ knew something sinister was going on. It was okay, though. He had already said goodbye to his father.

The double entrance doors swung open, and a wall of heavily armed men entered, stepping well inside to allow others to fill in the space behind them. It was instantly clear to everyone in the room that the men were there to take BenZ into custody.

Pilar clutched Sam's arm, and BenZ stepped to where they were standing. He put a giant hand gently on Sam's shoulder, all the while looking down at Pilar. He didn't speak. Tears as precious as raindrops in a land savaged by drought streamed down his big face, his eye color changing from green to sky blue. The whole assembly was silent. BenZ put his other hand behind Pilar, pulled her close and gazed into her eyes but said nothing.

When a guard at the front of the assembled force stepped forward to speak, BenZ took his hand from Sam's shoulder raised it high in the air as if to say, "Quiet." Making a whispering sound, he let his hand drop from Pilar, turned away from the armed men, and pushed open the doors to the veranda on the roof. As the people watched in astonishment, he strode quickly to the edge, stood still for a moment, turned to the crowd, raised his hand high in the air, waved goodbye, and disappeared over the side of the 40-story building.

Pilar cried out and Sam froze with disbelief. Shouts of surprise and concern rang through the crowd as the reality of what they had just witnessed hit home. The giant creature of so much world attention, the entity on which so much money had been spent to hear the wisdom he would offer had just jumped to his death.

Interface media caught the whole thing on video, even the fall, and cyber screams of indignation drowned out text explanations for what had transpired. Bold, flashing print appeared on the screens, asking why in the name of God such a thing had been allowed to occur. An immediate consensus of outrage focused on the insensitivity of the Bentley Administration.

Water Works

Benjamin Brand's face was contorted with tears of grief, and he could not bring himself to look at Marvin or the president. Weary from being so angry and so troubled, he could barely contain himself. Now, with the loss of BenZ and the work of a lifetime, he wasn't sure he could maintain decorum in the presence of the president, much as he was trying. Both she and Marvin appeared to be in a state of shock, neither having dreamt that the creature of their scorn would commit suicide rather than be taken into custody.

An urgent message for the CIA director flashed on an Interface screen in the Oval Office. The president nodded approval, and Marvin commanded, "Public display." Deputy CIA director Joseph Moss appeared and said, "Sir, a few hours ago, we arrested nine people in this country, and our allies have a dozen more in Pakistan. In addition, the Sephtis headquarters has been destroyed and we have confirmed that most of their top-tier leadership have been eliminated."

"Well, that's great news, Joe," Marvin said, glancing at Brand and smiling at the president.

"Sir, I wish that were the case."

"What do you mean?"

"It's the terrorists in custody, sir."

"Well? Are they talking?"

"Yes, sir. We can't shut them up. They are laughing and crying and dancing with leg irons."

"What are you saying, Joe?"

"I can hardly bring myself to tell you, sir. They now see themselves as martyrs. They say they will be dead soon and there is nothing we can do to stop it. They claim to have poisoned public water supplies here in Washington, and in Detroit, Dallas, Chicago, and Seattle as well. Also in Paris, London, Madrid, and Berlin."

"When did they allegedly do this, Joe?"

"About two weeks ago, sir."

"But we haven't had any reports of people being poisoned, have we, Joe?"

"No, sir, that's just it. They claim there is a delayed reaction, that it takes ten or twelve days after a person has consumed about three and a half gallons of water to take effect."

"What then, Joe?"

"Certain death, sir. No antidote."

"And when is this supposed to begin?"

"As early as tomorrow, sir. Where have you been getting your drinking water?"

Marvin and the president seemed frozen, locked in one another's gaze. After a long moment of silence, Brand heard himself saying, "Moral priorities, Madam President. Moral priorities. If you'd only had those men picked up when I gave you their locations, this would not be happening."

Retreat

I nterface news agencies all over the world exploded with reports about the appearance in America of the creature known as Benzeerilla. Typically, the headlines were sensational and overly dramatic: "Real King Kong Blasts Human Race," "Benzi-Frankenstein Speaks to the World, Calls Humans a Virus," "Ape-Man Lectures Humanity," "Benzeerilla Finally Speaks," and "Man-Monster Prophet of Doom."

"I'm surprised they didn't look for excuses to keep you here or lock you up," Sam said to Brand when they reconnected.

"President Bentley and the CIA are worried about other things right now. I'm not even on the list of their concerns anymore. In those last moments I had with the president, she was shouting at a White House staffer over the decision to use D.C. tap water in response to sporadic shortages. I will fill you in on the way home."

In the twenty-four hours since BenZ's death, Seth had spent much of his time with Pilar. He had watched her from across the room at the hearing and spoke to her for the first time on the street when he and Sam ran to the place where BenZ had fallen. Sam quickly introduced the two of them, and in the next moment, Pilar was sobbing uncontrollably in Seth's arms.

Now Seth, Sam, Pilar, and three of their security men were riding in a stretch limousine, with seats down as a makeshift hearse, to transport the body of BenZ to the airport where Brand had an aircraft waiting for the flight back to Peru. When Sam told Seth that Brand had invited him to come with them and use the time to finish his story, he accepted without hesitation.

The flight to Peru was a hushed, somber affair. Two days after the group landed, a funeral was held for BenZ. The body was placed in an above-ground crypt behind Brand's headquarters. On the third day, meetings began in the conference room to plan what to do next to make sure the legacy of Benzeerilla would be honored. It was clear, though, that they would have plenty of time to turn their plans into action, as the world was experiencing chaos.

More than two million people had died from water poisoning, not only in the major cities where the water supplies had been tainted, but sporadically all over the world because of visits to those cities by people who had consumed enough of the water before returning home. President Bentley was dead and so was her vice president. CIA director Marvin Winthrop was hospitalized in Washington and was expected to recover. His prognosis was good because he had not ingested a lethal amount of the poisoned water, only enough to be seriously ill.

The rapid accumulation of bodies with no efficient means of disposal was posing another major health risk all over the country. "It should be over in another week," the news reports said, but they would not speculate about how many would die before then.

In her room alone, Sam received an incoming Interface notice from BenZ. A screen opened, ceiling-to-floor, on three walls.

Soft music played in the background, and then BenZ appeared. His face was contorted, almost frozen sad. He said, "Samantha, Mother, I forgive you. I don't want you to feel guilty, ever. I think if you tell the world about your role, you will be subject to ridicule for a while, but in the long run, for you and the world, it will be a good thing. Always remember, I love you." Quietly sobbing, Sam watched the screen until it went dark.

On the morning of the fourth day, Brand asked everyone to meet in the office. He had invited Pilar to stay on and work for him on special assignments. Having her around was a comfort to him because of her link to BenZ.

"I have some things to say this morning that are going to be hard for some of you to hear, but they must be said. I need to get these things behind me. Keeping them to myself is too painful."

"Before you start," Sam interrupted, fixing her eyes on Brand, "tell me how BenZ knew that I was his mother. How long did he know?"

"Sam, the better question might be how we ever kept anything from him that he wanted to know. He could read all of us like books with large print. He knew when we were lying, but he seldom took us to task for it."

With tears in her eyes, Sam slowly shook her head. "I am so sorry I never told him I was his mother, and the fact that he knew all along makes it even worse."

"You must not feel that way or blame yourself. It was my idea to keep it from him in the beginning, and he knew that. Before we went to D.C., BenZ and I had a long talk, after which I gave private orders to have the tomb out back constructed next to David's in our absence. I'm glad David was spared these recent events. I wish you could have known him, Seth."

Brand paused and studied his hands. After a long silence, he said, "This is the hard part, the secret that's been eating away at me. You see, the reason BenZ selected the top floor of the new Capitol Tower wasn't really because it had twelve-foot ceilings and large elevators. He chose it because his plan all along was to jump to his death."

Sam and Pilar gasped. Seth sat up with a start.

"That's the only way he would agree to go," Brand continued. "If I wouldn't set it up, then he would simply commit suicide here. And there was nothing, I mean nothing, that I could do to talk him out of it. Believe me, I tried. I was even going to slip him a tranquilizer, medicate him, and try to change his mind, but I knew in the end it wouldn't work.

"BenZ kept telling me, over and over, that it was simply not possible for me to comprehend the loneliness of being the only one of his kind on the planet, and he wanted no others like himself created. As intelligent as he was, he could not control himself when he was angry. He grieved about the damage he did when he went on a rage, and he wanted this experiment halted. End of story.

"And here is something even harder for me to deal with. BenZ knew that his death would have an immortalizing effect on the words he left behind. He could see in my eyes that I knew this as well, and I could see confirmation in his. It felt like a ripping and tearing of the soul, if in fact there is such a thing."

"Then why didn't you tell me all this?" Sam whispered.

"Because he made me promise not to. I wanted to, Sam, but he said, 'Do not betray me on this, Father,' and I couldn't. Even so, he wanted everyone to know that you were his mother because he thought it would be better for you in the future. I'm not sure of the reasoning. It seems as strange to me now as it did then."

Tears were streaming down Pilar's face. "I wanted to talk to him. Why didn't he let me talk to him? Why didn't he communicate with me after he left?"

"It was just too painful for him, Pilar. With all the intelligence he possessed, he simply could not live with being alone in the world. I didn't allow for the fact that it would have such an effect. But I should have known, and BenZ reminded me often that I should have known. We tried to create a mate for him, but he would not condone it. There will be no more attempts by me to create another BenZ. My work from now on will be to simply show mankind how we might do some genetic tweaking that will make the time our species has left on this planet more meaningful and less harmful to the many other species over whom we have godlike power, as BenZ explained. I do not agree with BenZ's prediction that we are a doomed species, but when you consider his deep roots in the animal world, I can see why he felt the way he did."

Seth leaned forward in his chair and said, "When I had a session with BenZ in private, he said that in some ways he was as far advanced from humans as we are from our nonhuman primate cousins. But when I asked him for some examples, he just smiled and said I wouldn't understand. So, what occurs to me now is, if he was that far advanced, then why didn't he help engineer some scientific breakthroughs that would have advanced some of the things he thought we should do?"

"That's the undying question that's always been at the heart of our dilemma," said Sam.

"Yes, he was asked this question many times and in many guises," said Brand. "His not being forthcoming with good reasons was very inconsistent with his character. But Sam and I know why BenZ was so obstinate."

"Why, then?" Seth asked.

"Because he cared for us as individuals, but he despised humanity," Sam said.

"Here's what I think," Pilar volunteered. "If BenZ had been asked to describe someone else behaving that away, he would have said that reluctance to admit one's smoldering contempt is a very human thing to do." She smiled with confidence, knowing she'd put icing on the cake.

Getting up from his chair, Brand said, "BenZ has left us volumes of aphorisms and hundreds of hours of video lectures that we can make available to the public. In January, we will publish a calendar worldwide through Interface media that will be titled *Things Benzeerilla Said*. His legacy will live on.

"Oh, and Seth, BenZ wanted you to take care of Max. That dog meant a lot to him. Watching BenZ and Max, you could swear they were communicating, not with sounds but just with facial expressions. We have lots of video to study of the two of them interacting that I trust you will find astonishing."

When Seth happily jumped to his feet to shake hands, Brand added, "Sam tells me you had a dog that looked just like Max and that you are good with animals. That's encouraging because Omar says first you need to coax Max away from BenZ's tomb and get him to eat."

•◆•

Pilar had been spending more and more time with Seth in recent days, but after the meeting, she wanted to be alone. When she shut the door to her room, an Interface message appeared and the lights dimmed. Soft music began to play, a barely audible rendition of Rachmaninoff's second piano concerto, her favorite, introduced by her mentor. BenZ's face filled the screen. He was smiling. "Hello, Pilar," he said. "I am happy now. I am free and so are you."

He spoke for ten minutes, and when it was over, the Interface screen went blank but the music rose and continued. Cherishing his words of reassurance, Pilar smiled through her tears.

EPILOGUE

Marvin Winthrop resumed his post as director of the CIA, and redundant measures were put in place to protect the nation's water supplies. Almost five million people had died during what Interface media had begun calling Hemlock November. The number would have been much higher, but the Centers for Disease Control came up with an effective treatment that saved thousands. Marvin described the experience as a great moral awakening, because the grief felt all over the world had put human differences in a new perspective that begged for reverence. He hoped that, in the future, the world would be much better at establishing moral priorities.

With the president and vice president both dead, the speaker of the House of Representatives, Cheryl Tompkins, a liberal, was sworn in as U.S. president. She vowed to bring the country together in a way that would honor both conservative and liberal ideologies without either side feeling oppressed. For all practical purposes, the organization known as Sephtis had been destroyed, but the new president made clear that when or if new uprisings appeared, they would be dealt with swiftly and harshly.

Samantha Tyson was now Samantha Brand. Benjamin turned his laboratory attention to genetically engineering minor changes in fetuses to result in major advantages for individuals and society at large. At the same time, he began developing new antibiotics to combat superbugs and viruses.

Seth and Pilar were married on the first day of summer in 2044, in an outdoor ceremony at the Kudzu Zoo. They exchanged vows in front of a giant steel frame of Benzeerilla with fresh-cut kudzu filling the interior. A sleeping Rottweiler lay at the base. Nearby, an Interface terminal with a rain roof featured a biography of Benzeerilla narrated by Pilar, along with videos of his lectures on various subjects.

The Kudzu Zoo was so successful that Pilar's family moved to Tennessee to help run and maintain the place. The newlyweds had decided they would live in Tennessee during the summer and fall, and would spend the winter and spring in the Peruvian village near the Brand headquarters, where both would work on BenZ projects.

On the Brand Interface, a video montage was available for viewing, accompanied by these words:

"Benzeerilla was my mentor. He taught me to value every minute of every day that I draw breath. The ability to live with full comprehension and appreciation for our lives, right up to the point of our own demise, may be unique in the universe. Even though humanity is on a path toward species annihilation, a worthwhile existence is still available to all individuals for the taking.

"Benzeerilla taught me that kindness is a core expression of appreciation for one's life that can extend to every form of life. It is the only avenue of connection with all life. He taught me how to think beyond my cultural upbringing as a key to personal fulfillment. Not to pursue this level of consciousness is to forever exist as an expression of ideas that are not one's own.

"By American standards, the village I grew up in was poor, but I've learned that to be poor applies less to economics than it does to knowledge acquired and how we apply it in gaining perspective about our place in time. The knowledge that puts one person's life into perspective with all of life is what has always been missing from humanity's dominion over the earth.

"BenZ was in every way superior to us, and yet he said we already have wisdom enough to live a good life if we but pay attention. He asked me to memorize this quote from Ralph Waldo Emerson's essay 'Compensation':

> The same dualism underlies the nature and con-
> dition of man. Every excess causes a defect; every
> defect an excess. Every sweet hath its sour; every
> evil its good. Every faculty which is a receiver of
> pleasure has an equal penalty put on its abuse. It is
> to answer for its moderation with its life. For every
> grain of wit there is a grain of folly. For everything
> you have missed, you have gained something else;
> and for everything you gain, you lose something.
> If riches increase, they are increased that use them.
> If the gatherer gathers too much, nature takes out
> of the man what she puts into his chest; swells the
> estate, but kills the owner. Nature hates monopo-
> lies and exceptions.

"BenZ said that until you can begin to see the world with this kind of penetrating perception, you cannot experience what we teach as maturity.

"Near the end of his talk in Washington, D.C., on October 31, 2043, BenZ was asked what kind of advice he had for ordinary people. His reply was to learn more and more about the world until the people whose company you keep begin to think you live in another world. He made this point to me often. To seem out of touch is the only way to be in touch to the point of being able to see the cultural strings that make puppets out of citizens.

"I will say to you what BenZ used to say to me: Learn more and more about the world until you can see the strings. While this may sound cruel, you will come to realize that, once you truly understand the cultural strings that bind us, only time can free us.

"Thank you and the best of luck. Pilar Shepard, July 4, 2044."

About the Author

CHARLES D. HAYES is a self-taught philosopher and one of America's strongest advocates for lifelong learning. He spent his youth in Texas and served as a U.S. Marine and as a police officer before embarking on a career in the oil industry. Alaska has been his home for more than forty years.

Hayes' book *Beyond the American Dream: Lifelong Learning and the Search for Meaning in a Postmodern World* received recognition by the American Library Association's *CHOICE* magazine as one of the most outstanding academic books of the year. His other titles include *Existential Aspirations: Reflections of a Self-Taught Philosopher*; *September University: Summoning Passion for an Unfinished Life*; *The Rapture of Maturity: A Legacy of Lifelong Learning*; *Training Yourself: The 21st Century Credential*; *Proving You're Qualified: Strategies for Competent People without College Degrees*; and *Self-University: The Price of Tuition is Desire. Your Degree is a Better Life*. His fiction work includes the novels *Portals in a Northern Sky* and *A Mile North of Good and Evil*, and the novellas *Pansy: Bovine Genius in Wild Alaska*, *Stalking Cindy*, and *The Call of Mortality*.

Promoting the idea that education should be thought of not as something you get but as something you take, Hayes' work has been featured in *The L.A. Progressive*, *USA Today*, and the *UTNE Reader*, on National Public Radio's *Talk of the Nation* and on Alaska Public Radio's *Talk of Alaska*. His web site, www.autodidactic.com, provides resources for self-directed learners—from advice about credentials to philosophy about the value that lifelong learning brings to everyday living. In 2006, Hayes established www.septemberuniversity.org, a site devoted to ongoing dialogue among September University participants in search of the better argument.

Amazon Kindle versions are available for all the books mentioned above.

www.ingramcontent.com/pod-product-compliance
Lightning Source LLC
Chambersburg PA
CBHW022154260626
47155CB00018B/1925